New World

Undead Book 2

The Apocalypse Chronicles

by Jon DeLeon

Table of Contents

For Sarah

Chapter 1

Naval Air Station Key West: Outbreak Day +3

I promise. Last night, Joe had promised Kira to come back. He had never made a promise like that. It was considered bad luck. To commit to something after a tour or make a promise of return was almost signing your death certificate. A new level of nervousness rose from Joe's gut and burned in his throat.

Joe walked along the connected boats' back decks. He was leaving Kira and the kids. He would rejoin the military, do what he could to save others. It was his job. Still, it was one of the hardest walks he'd taken.

Joe hopped into a jeep that had been sent from Naval Air Station Key West. He had been in communication with a fellow officer at the base, relaying all the intel he could about his personal interaction with the undead. The air station had been running raids and rescue missions the past two days. Their efforts had saved the lives of many and drawn a line of farthest advance for the zombie threat. The islands were connected by only one road, which created bottlenecks with each bridge. The southern islands, which remained free of Enerjax, had been cut off from the northern islands for protection by blocking a bridge farther north.

Upon arrival at the base, Joe was taken to the base commanding officer's office.

"Colonel, you asked to see me?"

"Yes, come in." Inside was a mix of wood and brick. A touch of class in an older, cheaply built room.

"Captain, I'm told you have special training in exfiltration, more specifically in airborne extraction."

"Yes, sir." Joe had trained in Special Forces with a focus on rescuing or live capturing of high-value targets.

"Good. I need you to lead a team to rescue anyone you can from the Keys north of here."

"Of course, but why do you need my expertise, sir?"

"When this 'outbreak' started, we didn't know what the hell was going on. It took us a few hours to figure it out. By that time, we needed a strong response. We aren't a major hub down here. Over the past years, our numbers have been cut drastically. We did the only thing we could really do. We cut ourselves off and protected what we could until more forces arrived." The colonel stood up and pointed at a map on the wall. "North of here is Cudjoe Key. We took out the bridge between Cudjoe and Sugarloaf."

"You took out the bridge?" Joe had expected a roadblock and gun positions.

"Yes, we had to set up an operationally sound base. We have the equipment to rebridge to the island,

and now, thanks to the recent arrival of two crew ships, we have the men. We are going to repeat the actions we took. The plan is to blow the bridge connecting Cudjoe and Summerland, the Key to the north of Cudjoe. Rebridge to Cudjoe and sweep it of any threats. Once done, we repeat with the next one."

"Island-hopping."

"Exactly."

"Seems like a sound plan. Why do you need aerial extraction then?"

"It's going to take time to island-hop, and we are receiving distress calls from Keys several hops away. I won't leave innocents out there to die simply because we must move carefully. So I'm sending you. Look, the truth is, we are building a new America. Hell, it's a new world. This is a process of rebuilding and regaining territory one island at a time, but for those people out there, it's a matter of holding on and praying that their time doesn't run out before we can get to them. You can get there and bring them here. Every soul you rescue, not only are you going to be protecting lives but you'll be providing hope for the people here that something else survived. That it's possible somewhere down the road to reclaim a sense of normal. That sense of normality is the best hope we can strive for."

"What's the plan, sir?" Joe asked.

The colonel stood up and walked to a very official-looking map of the Keys that was hanging on the wall. He pointed as he talked. "Currently we are here on Key West. As I mentioned, we cut ourselves off and will be island-hopping. The order of operations is as follows. Naval forces tactically blow the bridge to the north of the next island in the chain. Now that it is completely cut off, we have control of the island. Snipers and mounted technicals from boats clean up any undead we can see. Once they are done, the engineers will bring the bridging equipment up and close the gap in the southern bridge, allowing us to have access. Ground forces and vehicles will enter the island and completely sweep it of undead. Once it's clear, we move on to the next island. While this is happening, you and your team are flying on rescue missions farther north. Any questions?"

"Where did you get all the bridging gear from?"

"Luckily enough, we actually had a stockpile of it in a warehouse here on base. It was being phased out, and we were tasked with destruction and reclamation of the materials to be turned into reef-building material. Part of a project for military resources to help reinvigorate the marine life here."

"That's lucky."

"Well with everything that happened, I guess we have to get one."

"Yeah, so what's my job exactly, sir? I have worked with all the branches in multiple roles in my career so far, so where do you need me?"

"Well when you radioed in, we checked your file on the databases that are still running for the meantime, and it says you're airborne. Is that correct?"

"Yes, sir, among other things." Joe adjusted his seated position to better show the colonel his Special Forces, Airborne and Ranger tabs.

"Good. We have people. We have a few soldiers, marines and seamen but not many officers. I need you to command a unit."

"Yes, sir. If I may, what happened to all your officers?"

"Unfortunately when all this mess started, two of the enlisted men who were working in the officers' mess had taken some Enerjax in order to feel more awake. Well they started a rampage wave of zombies that would have overrun the base if it wasn't for a little luck. I was on my way to the mess when I heard something going on. I looked through the window to see the zombie corpses of my men rising from the dead. I did the only thing a person could do. I jammed a pole through the door handles and corralled a firing squad. We ended that outbreak in time. Unfortunately we also lost most of the commanders. Which is why you're needed."

"When do I start?"

"Now. The man outside will take you to your team. We don't have much time before we lose the light."

The commanding colonel walked to the door. Joe followed suit.

"Good luck."

Joe left the office with a little extra pep in his step. He knew what was happening out there. If people were alive and trapped, they didn't have much time.

Florida Keys: Outbreak Day +3
8:00 a.m.

The chopper whined as the sea and ground flew by outside. Joe and his three-man team were headed north to Islamorada. A man had radioed down from his boat about a family he could see trapped on the roof of a restaurant in town. From his accounts, the undead were working on tearing the building down. Apparently the horde had given up trying to climb and decided to bring their prey to ground. That idea frightened Joe. If the zombies were still somewhat intelligent, that meant they were more dangerous than he had thought. Hopefully this eyewitness account had simply been wrong.

As the helicopter approached the location sent in from the fishing vessel's captain, Joe saw his worst fears coming true. There was the family trapped on the roof of the building. They were only a few hundred feet from shore, but it may as well have been a mile. Hundreds of zombies swarmed in a slowly rotating mass of undead human flesh. The restaurant was built on stilts, like many island structures. It was impossible to tell from above what the horde was doing beneath the building, but the occasional wood bracing flew from under it. The zombies were actually ripping the restaurant down to get served their meal.

Time was running out. The south side of the building was already beginning to sag. Joe and another man were winched to the roof. The family ran to them, tears and fear in their eyes. It was a grandfather, dad, mother and young son. The mother and son were pulled up first, followed by the grandfather and dad. Only after a quick canvas of surrounding windows and rooftops did Joe and his man clip into the winch.

The helicopter turned south and began heading home, with its occupants safe. Joe watched out the window as the building fell, engulfed by the zombie horde. A loud wail climbed into the sky, the zombies clearly upset their meal had gotten away.

Joe and his men dropped off their human treasure and left, again heading north for another run.

La Vida Dulce: Outbreak Day +3

Joe had just gone out of sight when Kira, who had woken early after hearing his boot steps, broke down crying. The weight of the world now fell on her shoulders, but she would keep her promise too; she would protect these kids.

Kira was watching three small mouths eat breakfast with sad looks on their faces. She was staring. Kira didn't know what to do. Two days ago, she had been an assistant at a yacht sales office. The greatest responsibility she had ever held was not losing the keys to an expensive boat. Now she had to provide and care for the lives of these kids. Who was she to take this on? She wasn't ready to be a mother, even for a couple days.

"Miss Kira?"

Kira had been staring at her bowl of cereal, which had now turned into a lump of mush. Elizabeth had broken her trance.

"Yeah, yeah, Elizabeth?"

"Jack needs to change."

The little boy had spilled some milk down his shirt. He was just learning how to eat with a grown-up spoon. *Thank God he was potty trained*, thought Kira.

"Oh okay, then let's . . ." Kira realized mid-sentence that the children didn't have any extra clothes. Neither did she, for that matter. "Okay, girls, will you help me put our dishes away? Then we can go find your brother some new clothes."

The little girls put the bowls in the on-board dishwasher and rinsed their hands in the sink. In the meantime, Kira wiped the boy's shirt with a towel. The milk spill still showed, but at least it would dry faster. Kira helped the children put their shoes on and got ready to leave.

"Do you guys know the hand-holding rule?"

"Yes!" Elizabeth beamed with pride. "I hold Chrissy's hand and yours, and you hold Jack's!"

"Don't call me Chrissy." Christine pouted.

"Okay, Christine. Now everyone hold hands," Kira interjected.

Together they left their new home and headed toward the mainland.

Key West: Outbreak Day +3

Kira had a few missions on this trip to the mainland. First they needed to find some clothes for the kids, and then they needed to find a way to get fuel. During their raid of CVS in South Beach, they had procured enough food and medicine to last for weeks, but without gas, the boat wouldn't provide fresh water or be very comfortable living quarters.

Finding clothes for the kids turned out to be easy. The economy on the island had gone back to simple bartering. It had cost Kira her gold earring just to buy herself a pair of jeans, ill-fitting sweatpants and a few tank tops and sets of underwear. The kids' clothes came free. The shop owners lit up at the sight of a group of young, well-behaved kids. Kira suspected they thought she was the now-single mother of the trio and took pity on her. She didn't care. After each of the girls and Jack had five or six changes of clothes, she set her sights on finding a way to get gas.

After a few hours waiting in line, she reached the front. She filled out the paperwork, interrupted a few times by one of the kids trying to wander off, and handed it back to the man. The man sitting at the table handed her a number. "What's this?" Kira asked.

"Show up here tonight at 6:00 p.m., and you'll be issued a fuel canister with your daily allotted rations. Make sure you keep track of your canister. In the morning, bring it back here, and I'll give you a number again. No can, no number, no gas. Got it?"

Kira nodded yes. Elizabeth did the same, trying to seem more grown-up. Kira and the kids went back to the boat and put on their new change of clothes. At 5:00 p.m., Kira turned on the television and put in the DVD of some animated movie. The yacht dealer had stocked every boat with the movie to entertain children while taking their parents on test rides.

Kira made her way to the fuel line and got into position. She felt like she was on a broken escalator. Step forward, stop. Step forward, stop. Again and again for about an hour, until she reached the front. There were lines of fuel cans. One was a ten-gallon container, while the other was twenty gallons. Kira handed the man her number card, and he reached down for a ten-gallon container.

"Wait, how come I don't get the twenty gallons? We have a larger boat."

"Do you have a catch to trade in?" the man handing out fuel asked.

"A catch?" Kira asked.

"Fish, crab, conch?" the man asked, more annoyed.

"Well no," Kira said.

"Then you get the ten gallon." The man shoved the can into Kira's stomach. She stumbled back a few steps. "Next."

Kira turned, shocked and hurt, and started walking home. "Hey, wait up a minute."

A young man ran up behind her carrying his twenty-gallon container. "My name's Hank. What's yours?"

"Kira."

"I saw what happened. I want to help," Hank said.

"How?" Kira asked.

"I have a fishing boat. I go out in the morning and come back before lunch. Yesterday I brought in two times the catch amount. You help me catch more fish, and I'll split some of the catch with you. Then you can get more gas."

"Really?"

"Yeah. Look, you help me catch more so I can barter more, and you get more gas. It's a win-win."

"I haven't fished in a while."

"It's all good. It's easy around here. Look, my boat is the *Conte Cristo*. It's docked right there." Hank pointed at a small, inflatable, zodiac-style boat that was tied to the pier. "See it? It's nothing big, but it's fast and lets me fish easily. Show up at 5:00 a.m. tomorrow, and we'll hit the waves. Don't trust me? Here, I'll trade you my gas canister. I have extra fuel right now anyway. Take it, come back if you want."

"No, thanks, I don't need the gas that badly," Kira said, wary of this man she didn't know and of owing favors.

"Don't be foolish. This is just a gift," Hank said.

"What's the catch?" Kira asked.

"Grouper." Hank said, smiling.

"You know what I mean," Kira said, not amused.

"No catch, really. I believe in helping those in need. If my heart calls me to give, I do, and it's telling me to help you out and that you're a good soul."

Kira wrinkled her brow.

Hank got serious. "Do you have someone you survived all this zombie stuff with?"

"Yes," Kira answered, "I have three small children and a man."

"Well those close to me didn't survive," Hank said, pausing to control his emotions. "All I ever had was my father, really. He was an abusive drunk, and most of the time, he smelled of liquor. I hated him, but I also loved him. Well he got bit. He turned. I . . . I had to kill him myself. At first I was happy. I felt like God finally was paying him back for everything he had done to me, but then, well, I started to miss the bastard. Without him, I'm completely alone. The zombie plague left me more alone. Everyone is so retreated into themselves and hardly talking. I get it. We're all still coping, but I could just use someone to talk to. Out there on the ocean, it's peaceful, but while I'm sitting there, it's so mind-numbingly boring. I just could use company, someone to talk to while sitting out there. After that, I sell my fish, try to get supplies and sleep until the next day. Seriously, please come tomorrow. Just go fishing with me once. We'll be home so early with two of us, so it will only be a few hours, max. I'd bet your kids aren't even up yet by the time you come back."

"I help you fish, that's it. We clear the nets when we reach the quota for each of us to receive the larger fuel portion, and we come home."

"Absolutely," Hank answered.

"Okay."

"Okay?" Hank said, clearly excited.

"Okay," Kira said.

"Awesome!" Hank said. "I promise you will not regret this. I'll see you tomorrow."

Hank walked past Kira and headed toward his boat.

At least some people are still human around here, Kira thought.

Kira shot an evil eye at the gas distributor and walked home. She needed to get a good night's sleep before tomorrow's fishing trip. If they caught enough fish fast enough, she would be able to come back before the kids were up and about.

Key West: Outbreak Day +4

4:30 a.m.

Kira got up and quietly made her way to the kids' bedroom. They were all sharing the larger queen bed in the VIP guest room. It made them feel safer being together. All three children were still fast asleep. Before tucking them in, she told them she was going fishing and would try to bring back lunch. Kira had taken the king bed in the main room, with Joe's absence. She didn't know when he would be back again. She peeked in the other guest cabin, hoping to find Joe in one of the beds, but they were empty.

Kira put on the jeans and a tank top and headed out the back door to the marina. Hank was already prepping for the morning's fishing trip when Kira arrived.

"Morning! I wasn't sure you were going to show up."

"Yeah, well I need the extra gas."

"Well I guess we better get going then, huh? Hop in."

Kira stepped onto the boat and sat down. Hank untied the last rope and started the engine. Together they set out of the marina and headed to Hank's favorite fishing grounds. After about four hours of fishing, Kira and Hank had pulled in the catch requirement for both of them plus a few more. "Is it always this easy?" Kira asked as she cast out her line again.

"This is the secret fishing spot my dad found years ago. See?" Hank pulled out a notebook and flipped through the pages until he found a list of GPS numbers. "This location is the third on the list. If the fish weren't here, they would be at one of these other locations. My father figured it out years ago, before he died." Hank put the book back in the tackle box it had been removed from.

"Thanks for bringing me here. How much more fish do we need before heading back in?"

"What do you mean?"

"Well I came out with you, and pretty soon we'll have plenty of fish for you to barter with, so when do we go back?"

"About that . . ."

Kira looked at Hank with suspicion. His demeanor had changed.

"Look, this is my boat, and if you want to keep your catch, then you're going to have to do something for me."

"What?"

"Well you know, I'm a man and you're a woman. We both have needs. You needed a fishing job, and I need something a little more physical."

"No. We aren't going to do that."

"I don't think you understand."

"Oh no, I get it, I'm just saying that's not happening."

"And I'm not asking."

Hank put his hand on top of Kira's. She pulled her hand away with a forceful jerk. The ocean surrounded Kira. There wasn't a soul in sight. She may as well have been in a hidden room. She was trapped.

Hank grabbed her, threw her down onto the deck of the boat and took position over her. Kira knew she was overmatched if she tried to fight him, so she started looking around for a weapon.

"Look, it doesn't have to be this way," Hank said.

Kira struggled against his grasp, writhing violently. As she fought, she scratched at him and bit his arm. Hank reeled back and slapped her across the face, sending her to the deck of the boat.

"Trust me, you're going to like this. You're never gonna forget me."

Hank whipped off his belt and threw it to the side. He started to unbutton his pants.

Kira turned her head, crying. She was scared and didn't know what to do. She saw Hank's belt, which had been discarded. She heard the unzipping of his pants but didn't notice it. Kira had eyed something she needed. On Hank's belt was his fileting knife. She needed a free hand. Hank let go for a second to remove his shirt, giving her the chance she was looking for.

Hank was busy pulling his shirt over his head. Kira struck. She reached, grabbing the knife's hilt and pulling it free from its sheath. She plunged the knife deeply into his chest, twisting as she lost her balance in the rocking boat, its float disrupted by her violent move. Her aim, although accidental, was perfect. Hank fell dead over the side of the boat and into the ocean, a pool of blood spreading wide.

La Vida Dulce: **Outbreak Day +**
11:30 a.m.

Elizabeth ran up the half-flight of stairs at the sound of the door to the yacht opening. Kira walked in and set down a bag. Elizabeth ran and gave her a hug around the waist.

"Elizabeth, oh, it's good to see you."

"You're late. I though you left us too."

"Oh, of course not sweetie, and remember, Joe will be back. I actually have a surprise." Kira pointed at the bag.

"What is it?"

"Why don't you take a look?"

Elizabeth opened the bag and cheered. Inside was a stack of coloring books and crayons. "Thank you, Miss Kira!"

"They're for everyone. Go show your brother and sister."

"Okay! Oh, and Miss Kira?"

"Yeah, Elizabeth?"

"You stink." Elizabeth held her nose.

"You're right, Elizabeth."

Kira followed her downstairs and hopped in the shower.

The water ran down her face and naked body, but Kira barely felt it. She stared at her hands. She couldn't stop them from shaking. They were moving of their own will. The adrenaline of the morning was starting to flush out of her system with the water that went down the drain. Now shock was starting to take over. Her legs grew weak, and she couldn't stand any longer. She sat down on the shower floor, out of the water, just sitting in the coldness. Kira began to cry. She clutched her face in her shaking hands. Soon her whole body was shaking as silent tears poured out of her face. As she began to calm down, she looked at her hands. There was still blood under the fingernails. The red brought her mind back to her.

What have I done? I killed a man. I am a murderer. I . . . I . . . I don't feel guilty. What does that say about me? Am I like Dexter? Am I the next mass murderer? How can I not feel bad? I feel bad that I don't feel bad. Is that normal? I wish Joe was here. He would know what to say. I'm sure he's killed people. Never in cold blood though. Joe. What will he say if he finds out? Will he kick me off the boat? Will he take the kids away? Should he? I did just kill someone and then go and buy crayons. What is wrong with me? How can I smile and be so happy with Elizabeth right after I did that? I mean, I feel like he deserved it though. I guess it was just self-defense. I only killed him because he tried to rape me. Yeah. Killing him wasn't my choice. He made me. He may as well have committed suicide. Besides, the sharks will clear away the evidence, right? It doesn't matter. This is his fault. Fucking Hank. He made me.

Kira had stopped crying as her sadness turned into just anger. Her emotions had hardened. Kira stood up and looked at her hand. It sat perfectly still.

Kira finished washing the smell of fish and blood off her. After she was finished, she got dressed and went about making the kids' lunch. Out the window, she could see the *Conte Cristo* tied to *La Vida Dulce*. That bastard had tried to rape her. Instead he was dead, and she got another boat and a way to provide for the kids. At least karma still existed in the zombie apocalypse.

Southern Mainland Florida:
Outbreak Day +16

A long list of successful missions down, Joe had one more to go before a mandatory twenty-four-hour rest period. The commanding officer had imposed it after the last mission. What should have been an easy roof grab like the rest had turned chaotic when the undead mass broke through the gate leading from the fire escape. Joe and one of his men had each emptied three magazines into the line of zombies before they could clip onto a rope and be pulled airborne by the rising chopper. These were the first shots they had needed to fire. They had gotten unnecessarily close to dying.

The current mission was to investigate a strange signal. They were heading farther north than they had ever gone, all the way up into mainland Florida. A signal had been picked up, calling for survivors to rally. If it was true, this would be a place in need of protection and possibly rescue, or even an ally to connect with.

As the chopper approached the source of the signal, its transmission came through clearly. The pilot put the transmission over the radio system.

"Survivors! Come! We have food and supplies. The end is here! The world is new. You are free from your old restrictions, your old restraints. Come to Johnny's Funworld and enjoy the new world. Get your rocks off with a beautiful woman for cheap. You know you've always wanted to. Now there is no police force stopping you from being yourself. It's time to enjoy the ride."

The signal repeated continuously.

The pilot came over the intercom. "Sir, are you hearing this?"

Joe answered back in disbelief. "Roger. Let's just rescue those we can."

"Yes, sir."

The helicopter set down in a clearing to the west of the building sending out the signal. Joe and his fire team covered the final quarter-mile by foot. The building was one story tall and rectangular in shape. Out front was a carnival tent that draped over the main entrance door on the side of the building, with a green military canopy a few hundred yards away. As Joe approached the carnival-looking tent, a man dressed in a purple velvet pantsuit stepped out.

"Welcome, weary travelers! Welcome to Johnny's Funworld! Come in, rest your weary feet and spend a little time with a lovely young woman." The man did a little dance, motioning them forward with an evil smile on his lips.

"We aren't interested, sir. We are here to rescue you."

"Thanks, but I don't need you to rescue me. I'm doing just fine."

"Sir, I don't think you understand. We are pulling you and the women out of here."

"Look, Captain, we have plenty of water and food in the green tent, and we are safe. People come and leave. This is an important place for people to stock up before moving on."

"I understand that. Which is why we are going to leave a transmission running and the supplies, but we are taking you and your women to a safer area."

"Listen, for the last time, we don't need rescue. We are safe. God is on our side. He is watching down, protecting us."

"I respect your faith, but—"

"I am doing God's work here!"

"Calm down."

"I am doing God's work!" Johnny threw a wild punch, which Joe easily dodged.

"Okay, that's it." Joe turned to one of his men. "You, secure him. Everyone else, secure the area, look for survivors in the supplies tent or the surrounding area." Joe then looked at a young specialist named Martinell, whom Joe had been impressed with because of his amazing accuracy. Joe had seen him pick off zombies with perfect shots between the eyes, firing from the hip, multiple times. Martinell was the kind of man you wanted next to you at all times. Pointing to him, Joe said, "Martinell, you're with me. We're pulling the women out of that building."

"We don't need rescue!" Johnny yelled as he shoved him to the ground. He was quickly restrained using a pair of zip ties. "We don't need rescue!" Spittle flew from Johnny's mouth as he spat out his words at Joe, face in the dirt.

"I've got him, sir," the soldier holding Johnny said, tightening his hold by placing a knee in the irate man's back.

"Let's go, Martinell," Joe said.

"Wait!" Johnny yelled, somewhat more composed. "You can't go in there!"

"Why not?" Joe asked, clearly annoyed by this man.

"You have to take the magic pills first! They are in my pocket! It's the rule!"

Joe looked suspiciously at Johnny, turned away from him and walked toward the building. "Let's go, Martinell, and stay alert. Something's wrong here."

"No!" The muffled yell of Johnny fell on deaf ears, and Joe and Martinell strode toward the entrance to Johnny's Funworld.

Joe and Martinell took one step into the building before being assaulted by a reek of blood and gore.

Joe moved his hand over his mouth, sealing it, both fighting to keep the stench out and holding back his breakfast. Martinell and Joe both pulled their military scarves, shemaghs, over their faces to help keep the smell of rusty metal mixed with decaying flesh out of their bodies.

They walked slowly to the first door. Joe opened it and stepped inside, followed by Martinell. The walls and floor were covered in layers of dried blood. Hand marks and smears were easily visible on the floor and walls. "What the—"

Joe was interrupted by the sound of chains dragging against the tile floor. Next came a loud screeching yell from the dark corner in the back of the room.

"Sir?" Martinell asked.

Joe took a step toward the scream. Chains started ringing again. A female zombie came sprinting full speed at Joe. Before he could even react, a loud pop echoed in the small room. Martinell fired one round that split the zombie's skull into a million pieces. It fell into a crumpled ball.

Joe took a step forward and examined the now fully dead zombie. "She has a chain and collar around her neck."

"Sir, what is this place?" Martinell asked in confusion.

Joe stared in disbelief at the dead woman on the ground in front of him. Joe walked out and looked down the hallway. There were five more doors.

"They can't all be, can they?" Joe asked the air absentmindedly.

"Sir? Please, what is this place?" Martinell asked more forcefully this time.

"This is a feeding room." Joe answered in near disbelief. "This is a feeding building."

Joe looked at Martinell. Martinell's face was full of disgust. Joe's face echoed the sentiment. Joe hardened his look. "We need to clear the rest of it. Follow me, Martinell."

Outside, the other men heard the burst of gunfire ring from the building. They moved quickly to come to Joe and Martinell's aid. As they ran across the open field that separated the supplies tent from the carnival-draped building, they heard four more bursts of fire ring out. Just as they were about to rush in the door, Joe and Martinell exited the building, both with their shemaghs around their faces. The men, panting from their breakneck run, stopped. One asked, "Sir, what's the situation?"

Joe looked from them to Johnny and made a beeline in his direction, not answering the soldier's question.

"What did you do?" Johnny was clearly enraged. He was still being restrained in his zip-tie handcuffs, which his guard was holding tightly behind Johnny's back as he stood there.

Joe punched Johnny in the face. Blood poured from his nose and tears from his eyes as his nose broke instantly. The man holding Johnny let go as he turned to dead weight and fell to the ground.

Joe responded, cold and angry at the man regaining his bearings while fighting to come to his knees on the ground. "We put those things to rest."

"You killed my women?" Johnny screamed through the blood running over his lips. "They were instruments of justice! They were purifying the world."

"What are you talking about?" Joe screamed back at him.

"The unworthy," Johnny said like a bratty schoolkid.

"What does that mean?"

"The sinners who give in to their lustful desires deserve what they find in those rooms!"

"Sir?" Martinell asked, understanding but afraid to be right.

Joe spoke loudly, talking to Martinell but never changing his gaze from Johnny, who had now worked his way back to a standing position. "He was sending people in there, telling them that they would find hookers. Instead they were eaten."

"What? Sir, there's no way a guy is going in that building and not running for the hills. The smell alone would make them turn tail," Martinell said.

Joe looked at the ground for a moment and then looked back up at Johnny. "You said we couldn't go in without magic pills. You're not just tricking them. You're drugging people. What are you giving them?"

"Just something to make them happy in their last moments. A grace they don't deserve for their sins," Johnny said dismissively.

"And nose-blind, you sick fuck," Martinell said angrily.

"They are the sinners!" Johnny shouted at him.

A shot rang out. The man holding Johnny was sprayed with blood as the back of his skull burst into a million pieces. Martinell had split Johnny's skull between the eyes.

"Hold your fire!" Joe turned on Martinell, staring at him intensely. Martinell stared right back.

The man holding Johnny wiped his face, trying to clean the blood and brain matter off. "What the fuck?"

"Martinell!" Joe commanded. Martinell stared, unapologetic. "Burn that building to the ground. We erase this from the earth. Everyone else, clear that supply tent and burn this body. In ten minutes, we get out of this place."

Helicopter blades whirled through thick black smoke as the chopper carrying Joe and his men rose into the air.

Joe turned and looked down at the colorful carnival tent burning an acrid sheen into the sky. Johnny's Funworld was melting to the ground, thanks to a flare and forty gallons of diesel.

He thought to himself while looking at that strange scene. *What kind of world is this?*

Chapter 2

The Settlement: Outbreak Day +11
The stray ashes from last night's bonfire
crunched into black powder under Kurt's boot as he
paced around the fire. He walked around the ring of
seats that had been arranged around the massive pit
built for the weekly celebratory burns. He could still
smell the coals that smoldered at the center of the
rock circle from last night.

It had been an awesome first night in the camp.
Kurt had really enjoyed the bonfire. The laughter and
smiles. The feeling of being part of a community. Last
night, Kurt had worn a massive grin. Last night, the
world wasn't a zombie hell. No, sitting there watching
Liz dance and seeing her pure, white and genuine
smile had filled a piece of his heart that had been
empty since the outbreak began. Just to witness true
release of stress after the fear and terror that had
gripped him since outbreak day had been something
truly amazing.

As Kurt finished his circumnavigation of the
pit, he stood back where his short trek had started,
where Tyler now sat. Kurt looked at him, time
traveling to last night again. Tyler had been sitting on
that same log, watching Liz and the others dance too.

Kurt and he had been sitting next to each other, but Tyler's face showed he was having a very different experience. Kurt had thought that he must have been reading too much into it, but he still couldn't shake it. The smile on Tyler's face last night. It wasn't genuine. It wasn't pure. It was full of something else that made Kurt uncomfortable. There was a suspicious malice to it. Now looking at Tyler, there was nothing. He was so tired and cold, he sat in a half-awake haze, staring at the ground, hugging himself in an attempt to stay some kind of warm. Kurt shivered himself. It was cold.

They were waiting for Philip to come and give them the arranged tour of the survivors' camp. Liz would get her own tour with a different group a little later that morning. She had already been given her job. After being so personable with the group dancing last night, they immediately called dibs on adding her to their water-filtration team, or the "H20 crew," as they called themselves. Liz, Kurt and Tyler didn't ask what that meant, but Liz still enthusiastically signed up. Her later tour today let her sleep in, something both Kurt and Tyler were jealous of.

They had both been sitting or pacing near the fire, tired and cold, for almost twenty minutes now. Philip, the leader of the camp and their tour guide today, was late. Annoyed and bored, Kurt kicked a small rock. It sailed through the air and flew right past Philip's head. Kurt's face turned white with shock and apologetic embarrassment.

"That's one heck of leg," Philip said, readjusting his hunting cap. "Are you a kicker?" He was dressed in full camouflage. He wore a thick hunting coat and utility pants and carried a thermos full of coffee.

"My bad, sorry. No, never played football . . . just connected, I guess."

Philip shrugged. "You two look tired."

Tyler stood up from the log, stretching a crick from his lower back. "Yeah."

"Want some coffee?" Philip dug two plastic mugs from his pocket.

Kurt declined. Tyler accepted with vigor.

"Coffee was somewhat of a routine for me. Before going on the run, I would have three cups a day, minimum. I've been detoxing. We ran out of coffee the day I met Kurt." Tyler turned toward him. "Probably why I wanted to shoot you so much. Wasn't in a good mood."

"You better drink up then," Kurt said.

Philip filled one of the mugs and handed it to Tyler. Philip returned the other mug to his pocket. One sip and Tyler visibly regained his feeling of being alive. The warmth of the mug and its liquid treasure shot a river of comfort through his body. "Ah." He shuddered as a shiver of warmth and energy melted through his body.

"It's good stuff, right?" Philip had pride in his coffee.

"Perfect."

"Great, well let's get this tour going. I'm due to relieve my sons at the gate." Philip turned with a wave of his arm and began to lead Tyler and Kurt through camp.

Philip started with an enthusiasm only a tour guide with an immense pride for something he created could have. "This is the fire pit, obviously. You are parked third spot in, right in line with the West tree sign." Philip pointed at the pit and then the wooden "W" sign hanging from the tree as he spoke. "You're farthest from the fire, but you're new here, so that's just the way it goes. The rest of the homes are arranged in a semicircle following the fire, and the road is the bisecting border, with my home being the closest to the gate, right next to the road. You'll find water tanks to draw from if you go about midway between 'W' and 'N,' and midway between 'N' and 'E,'" Philip said, again pointing at the wooden signs.

"Are those compass directions?" Tyler asked.

"Yeah," Philip replied. "Sorry, I could have been more clear about that. The wooden signs with the letters equal the directions they represent. Um, what was I saying? Oh, that's right. Like I said, you'll find water reservoirs if you head straight out from the fire pit, going directly up the middle of West and North, and North and East. You'll also find some outhouses near those tanks, and we have another outhouse directly to the north, or about a hundred yards into the forest past the 'N' sign. They are port-o-johns, so they aren't exactly fancy, but they work. We do have one actual bathroom in a building to the south, across the road, but I'll show you that one in a minute here. That's the real bathroom for the camp. The plumbing still works, so we demand that all number two is done in that building. None of us wants this to turn into a shit camp." Philip chuckled at his own joke. "Also, we try to save the outhouses for the ladies and use trees in most cases. Oh, and no dumping of your RV waste. We really don't want to deal with that issue yet. So just don't use it, if you can help it. Got all that?"

"Yep," Tyler said, taking a quick break from the coffee he was slowly sipping.

"Yeah," Kurt said. "I am curious though. Where are you getting your water from?"

"Well we actually have a pump that is drawing from a local well. It's located directly past the 'E' tree over there," Philip answered.

"What?" Kurt exclaimed, alarmed. "You have to stop!"

Philip furled his brow.

"Before I started running, I saw a news story online. They were saying that the water was being contaminated."

"This isn't tap water Kurt," Philip said calmly. "It's a natural spring the Russians drilled a well into. Plus we have a filtration system that is pretty robust. As a matter of fact, I can tell you with certainty, we are okay. It hasn't been too long since this whole thing started, but when we first got here and formed this settlement, our water reserves were empty. So we've already been drinking the water for over a week now, and we're fine. So we're good. Heck, I even made the coffee with it."

Tyler choked on the sip he was taking. "How can you be sure we won't get sick off weird bacteria?" he asked, suddenly nervous.

Philip laughed, "Ha ha ha, let me show you." He led Kurt and Tyler on a short walk toward the road. When he reached the road, he began to talk as he walked across it at an angle, heading past his own home, to the other side and into the opposing woods. "The well is there," he said, pointing into the woods to the northeast. "What we do is fill a designated reservoir, or water tank if you prefer easier terms, and label that dirty water. This tank here," Philip said as all three of them arrived at a plastic square container about four feet wide, four feet deep and four feet high with a metal grate surrounding it and a wooden sign with handwritten paint spelling 'Dirty' hanging on the side. Philip continued. "It's the job of some of our residents to pump the water from the dirty reservoir through the filter and into clean water reservoirs using this." Philip pointed to a hand pump that looked like an old-school railroad cart. "You can see the clean water tank is half-full. In most cases, this doesn't happen, but the bonfire tends to mess with the schedule. In any matter, today someone . . . actually I think your traveling companion and wife, if I understand correctly, will pump for the first time and fill the clean water talk up fully. Then the full tank will be taken out to the forest, where they replace the depleted water reservoirs out there. Those empty ones will be brought back and filled with clean water, and the cycle continues. That's how we have clean water nonstop. All that clear?" Philip asked.

"Yeah," Kurt said, nodding.

"Yeah, that solves the water problem. What about food?" Tyler asked, now more awake, thanks to the caffeine he was ingesting.

"Well let's take a walk down the road here." Philip led them a few hundred feet down the road heading away from the gate. "Here we have the grocery store." He pointed at a semi truck parked off the side of the road in a small open area where no trees had grown.

Tyler nodded and took another sip of his coffee. Kurt wandered around the back of the semi truck and saw a second one behind it, parked deeper in the forest. It was literally wedged in between two trees, head first. "Guess it doesn't need to go anywhere, huh?" Kurt said, looking at the scratch marks the trees had left as the semi had plowed between them.

"I assume they're locked," Tyler said after swallowing his sip of coffee.

"Yep," Philip answered. "Both the cabs and the trailers are locked with some heavy-duty master locks. I have the only sets of keys. Every week, on Monday, we all come together and divvy up supplies. The weekly allotment can be reduced for community infractions, like dumping your waste or missing assigned work duties. So we kind of have a built-in incentive to keep everyone working and in order, as well as rationing the best way and not running out of supplies too early."

"What's that?" Kurt asked while pointing at a bright-blue tarp tightly pulled over a stack of boxes in the forest, sitting on their own a few hundred more feet into the forest.

"That, my friend, is Enerjax," Philip said confidently.

"What?" Kurt and Tyler said in unison.

Well amazingly enough, it was on one of the trucks. So after realizing it was there, we separated it from the other items and even burned the boxes sitting closest to it, just to be safe. Luckily all we had to torch were lots of adult diapers. As for the Enerjax, we put it under that tarp to keep it away from us. We thought about trying to burn it, but we were afraid that the smoke may be just as dangerous, so we all agreed to put it way out in the forest. So stay away from it."

Kurt unconsciously took a step backward, away from the Enerjax pile. Tyler jumped behind Kurt and grabbed his shoulders, yelling, "Boo!" Kurt jumped nearly a foot in the air and took three running steps down the road before catching himself and regaining composure. Tyler and Philip were laughing so hard that they were nearly crying. Tyler said between laughs, "It's not gonna bite, man."

"You're a dick, man," Kurt said, catching his breath.

"Ha ha, that made my day. Come on, the best stuff is still to come," Philip laughed and said with a

massive grin on his face. Kurt rejoined Tyler and
Philip as they walked down the road, farther away
from the gate and fire pit. Philip pointed to his left as
they walked. "Here we have the fuel depot. We are
rich in gas. Four full tanker trucks. We don't really
need it much though. Not sure about you, but our RV
runs on propane for most of our electrical stuff."

Tyler responded, "Yeah, ours too. Actually
we're running low on that. I wasn't sure how much
longer the lights were going to stay on."

"Well that's pretty much why we chose to set
up here," Philip said proudly. "Follow me, boys." As
Philip led the three-person tour around a slight bend
in the road, they came upon a turnaround, and at the
far end sat a small brick building with large metal
pipes running to an industrial maze of small metal
pipes shooting into the ground and twisting around
each other. Several trucks with built-on round tanks
sat next to a pipe with a hose attached. The smell was
unmistakable.

"Is this a propane well?" Kurt asked, surprised.

"I know, right!" Philip exclaimed. "Not only is
it operational, but it pumps 24/7 into reserve tanks
under the ground. We came upon it, and luckily
enough, the Russian workers here, one of whom
spoke English, weren't sure what to do. Well my boys
and I originally had commandeered a second RV so
that we could each have a comfy bed. Well we traded
an RV and access to whatever supplies we find, like
food and water, and they stay here and keep the

system running. They man the facility and provide propane for all of us to use. Come on, let's go inside."

The trio entered the building. Philip waved to three men who sat behind a window on the right. They waved back at the group, smiling. After a quick wave, they turned back to a board of dials and readouts.

Philip pointed to a door at the end of the hall in the small building. "That's the shitter. Don't clog it, and close the door tight when you're done. Gotta keep the flies out."

A few minutes later, the three of them were back on the road outside and were walking toward the gate. Philip continued the narration of the tour as they slowly paced. "This way is the gate, as you already know. Basically the camp is a circle around the fire pit, and the supplies and resources are along the other side of the road here. Everything was put together pretty quickly, obviously, but it should be good enough to get us through the winter that is fast, fast approaching." Philip stopped walking as he stared into the sky for a second. "It's going to be cold."

Kurt broke his moment of thought. "Philip? Where did all this stuff and the people come from?"

Philip started walking again, heading now past the camp and nearing the gate. "Well the water tanks are ours. We had them and the pump to stay out here, well not here, but in Russia, and hunt the whole season while camping in our RV. Montezuma's revenge doesn't only happen in Mexico, you know. As for the people, semis, tankers and delivery trucks, day one of this outbreak was crazy. Once we found this place and made the deal with the propane workers, we drove down the road to the nearest intersection and flagged down anyone we could. The Russian propane workers gave us a simple map to the most densely traveled road, so we got a lot of attention. Then after a few days, we started hunkering down and putting up some tree roadblocks. At that point, we figured most of what would be coming down those roads would be either zombies or people we didn't want around. We had to make sure we stayed safe. I'm glad y'all made it though."

"Thanks," Kurt said. "What about the forest? How can you be sure we're safe from the forest?"

Philip smacked his head with his open palm. "Oh, I forgot to mention that to you. Obviously you're on the only easy way in and out of the settlement, this road. As you can see, we are almost at the gate that blocks the only way in or out on it, but the main protection of this camp is another blockade. This one is a huge ring of safety. If you were to walk out from the camp in any direction, a few hundred yards into the trees, you would find a web of barbed wire and strings with bells attached every so often. In one big circle encompassing the whole settlement. It's both a fence and an improvised early warning system. If anything human, zombie or animal comes through the forest, the camp will hear those bells ringing."

Tyler nodded his head and said with a surprised tone, "That's actually really smart."

"Thanks," Philip said. "I'm not sure if I should be flattered or insulted that you are surprised by my wisdom."

"As you can see, Kurt and Tyler, we have a pretty good system set up here. It's simple, but it works. Who knows, we may very well be the last of humanity."

"I hope that's not true." Kurt thought of his brother. He hoped that Joe had found a way out of Miami and was alive somewhere.

"Oh, don't get me wrong, I hope the world survives, but look around at the people in camp. We are the best of humanity. This apocalypse is just part of the cycle."

Kurt and Tyler both looked at Philip with confusion in their eyes.

"Think about it, both of you. The world went to hell. A new alpha predator emerged." Philip snapped his fingers with a loud pop. "Like that. In a matter of hours, we had only our instincts to guide us. Our animalistic traits buried deeply in our genetic makeup took over. Those who survive are the strongest and most cunning. It's nothing as trite and false as becoming a better salesperson or a beautiful movie star. This zombie plague is the real measure of a man. You made it. I made it. Those people in the camp made it. We are the new evolution of mankind."

There was a pause allowing Philip to bask in his impassioned speech.

The tour was over. It had ended at the gate.

Philip cupped his hands to his mouth and shouted, "Good morning, boys!"

Brandon and Jonathan climbed down the ladder of a tree stand that was barely discernible from the forest.

"You're late," Jonathan said, clearly grumpy. Brandon stood next to his brother, half-awake.

"Sorry, boys. I was giving Kurt and Tyler here a tour of their new home," Philip said.

Kurt and Tyler both nodded and said, "Hello."

Brandon said, "Welcome to your new home. Pretty cool place, huh?"

"Really, you want to start a conversation right now," Jonathan said, still grumpy. "I'm going to bed. Good night." Jonathan walked past them, pushing between Kurt and Tyler as he made his way down the road.

"He's just cranky cuz he's tired. Don't mind him. It's always good to have new people join the settlement," Brandon said.

"I'm taking the bottom bunk!" Jonathan yelled from down the road.

"I'll see y'all around," Brandon said to Kurt and Tyler. He ran after Jonathan, chasing him. "Bullshit!"

"Language!" Philip yelled at Brandon as he ran down road. Brandon raised his hand, waving it off.

Philip laughed. "What can I say? They take after their dad." He stood, staring down the road, watching his boys walking side by side, in a trance from his love and pride.

"So what now?" Tyler broke Philip's trance. Philip shook his head.

Philip snapped out of his trance. "Oh right. Well you go home and rest. Then you come back at three o'clock and relieve me of guard duty."

"What do we do if we come under attack?" Kurt asked.

"Shoot," Philip answered, laughing. "Don't worry about that though. We won't be attacked up here.

"How do you know that?" Kurt asked.

"The only people on this road are lost. No robbers come out here. There is nothing to steal. The zombies won't stick to roads either. They will walk from the closest cities, if they ever do, which are to the south. I didn't get to show you that side on the tour, but there is an extra ring on that side. That ring has pressure traps. Any undead coming all the way out here will be trapped. We are safe here."

"You sound pretty sure." Kurt wasn't entirely sold.

"I am," Philip said. "Now head back into camp. I'll see you both soon for your first guard shift. Go and get some food and a nap." Philip turned and walked into the forest, heading to the tree stand.

Tyler and Kurt walked back down the road to camp. When they got back to the RV, Liz was awake and cooking soup.

"Morning! Your timing is perfect. How does chicken noodle sound?"

"Chicken noodle? Where did we get such a delicacy?" Tyler asked.

"Agatha came over and gave it to us as a welcoming gift. She's giving me the tour in about an hour. I'll be working with her soon, doing water purification and pumping. She was telling me about it a little last night, but she'll give me the full details later today. Speaking of that, how was your tour? Does the place look nice?"

Tyler accepted a bowl and sat down at the table. "Coffee and chicken noodle soup, this is an awesome day! Yeah, the camp really does seem well set up, like a good system."

Kurt sat down as well. His response was not as peppy. "It's not bad, still not home though."

"We've got guard duty today. First day on the job," Tyler said after a big gulp of soup.

"Yeah, I'm going to pass on the soup and get some sleep," Kurt said.

"Should have had coffee," Tyler murmured.

"Maybe, but I'll take sleep today," Kurt said while lying down on the couch.

"Kurt, we're both up. Take the bed," Liz volunteered

"Great idea. You've never been in the bed yet, have you, Kurt?"

Kurt swallowed, a little awkward.

Tyler continued. "Go experience it. I'm sure you know, what's mine is yours. All you have to do is take it."

An awkward silence overtook the room.

"Don't say it like that. Now it sounds weird," Liz said.

"What? I'm just saying, he may as well enjoy everything, right?"

Kurt turned away, head into the couch, and went to sleep.

The Settlement: Outbreak Day +11

Kurt and Tyler walked up to the hunting blind overlooking the gate for their first guard duty. Tyler was bundled up in his warm clothes, while Kurt was in his winter jacket and jeans, carrying his entire backpacking pack with him.

Tyler yelled up to the blind, "Philip! Time for us to take over."

Philip climbed down the ladder a few seconds later. "You're on time! Good, I hate tardiness. Where are your guns?"

Tyler pulled out his pistol, showing it to Philip.

"Just a handgun? Well shit." Philip slung a rifle off his shoulder. "Here, take this hunting rifle too." He handed it to Tyler, who was closest. Tyler took it and handed the handgun to Kurt. Kurt tucked it in his coat pocket.

"Are you going on a hike, Kurt?" Philip asked, smiling playfully.

"He wouldn't come without it," Tyler said.

"I don't go anywhere without it. If I need to run, I'd rather be prepared," Kurt said equally as playfully.

"You're safe here. No need to lug that thing around. Here, hand it over and I'll carry it back to your RV," Philip said, taking a step toward Kurt.

Kurt stepped back. "Thanks, but I'll keep it." This time, his voice was purely serious.

Philip lowered his extended arm that had been reaching for the pack. "Suit yourself. Anyway, boys, enjoy your first guard duty. Albert will replace you at eleven tonight. There is a little solar-powered heater up there in the blind. Just don't move it much. It's finicky. You won't get too cold today, but eventually when you get a nighttime guard duty, you'll need that little heater. It gets cold, real cold. For now, just keep one eye looking outside for movement. Occasionally you'll see a deer or some other animal. If it's a good size, get it. Nothing better than a camp-wide feast. Just make sure you don't miss. That rifle is sighted well and shoots straight even with a cold barrel. Well boys, enjoy your guard duty. I'm going to figure out what my boys have gotten up to." Philip turned and headed down the road toward town.

Kurt took a seat on the floor and Tyler on a small camping stool that had been set up so the guard could sit and see easily out the window gap in the blind. Tyler looked around, nodding his head at the sturdy construction of the roof.

"Have you ever been hunting?" Kurt asked Tyler.

"Yeah, a few times, mostly when I was in high school. My dad, uncle and I went as a family-bonding experience, but always with a bow." Tyler laughed. "My dad used to say it was cheating to use a rifle. Didn't stop him from teaching us how to shoot though. What about you?"

"Nah, we went camping every once in a while, but that's about it. My brother and I used to go shooting but never got into hunting."

"Tell me more about you brother," Tyler said.

"Joe? What do you want to know?" Kurt asked.

"Anything, we have a lot of time to kill," Tyler responded.

"Well he's pretty much the man. He was always the sports star, always smart in general. And probably the thing I was most jealous of growing up, all the girls loved him. Even with a little jealousy and frustration when girls would come up to me and tell me to get him to call them or tell him they thought he was hot, we were always best friends. We were always there for each other. That's what made it hard when he went into the military. All of a sudden, he wasn't there, and I couldn't be there for him. It was just a vacuum that hasn't really ever been filled."

Tyler sat quiet for a moment, unsure of what to say. He decided to just ask another question. "What branch?"

"Army," Kurt answered, snapping out of a little funk. "He's Special Forces. So he's gone, most times doing crazy shit. Cool shit but crazy shit. Joe's always been a fighter. I was always the runner. If he was in

Miami when this all started, I'll bet he fought a bunch of zombies, probably saved some people."

"Kurt, if he is still alive, I'll make sure you find him."

"Thanks."

A minute of silence followed. Tyler hated silence, so he picked the conversation back up. "What's in that pack that is so important anyway? I told you Philip would give you shit."

"Yeah, you did." Kurt laughed. "It's just some camping gear, mainly backpacking equipment."

"Anything to eat? I just got real hungry for some reason."

"Actually yeah. I have a little stove and a few dehydrated soups at the bottom, if that sounds appetizing."

"You've been holding back! Set it up and cook us a snack."

Kurt set up the little single-flame stove and cooked a small pot of soup, pouring it into two metal mugs he had fished out of his backpack.

"Kurt, I know you want to be with your brother and all, but I'm glad you happened to cross my path. You're a good guy."

"Thanks, man," Kurt answered, holding his little metal mug out. Tyler clinked his metal mug against Kurt's. Together they sat watching the sun sinking lower on the horizon. Sunset on their first guard duty.

The Settlement: Outbreak Day +12

"Wake up, Kurt." Tyler nudged him awake.

Kurt was instantly pulled from a deep sleep. Tyler and Kurt had gotten back last night surprisingly tired from their first guard duty. Kurt had fallen asleep instantly and passed out hard. Tyler waking him up threw him into a slight panic.

"What's going on?" Kurt shot up ready to run, his heart racing.

"Whoa, calm down, man," Tyler said. "It's breakfast time. Liz left us some plates before leaving for her shift at the water pump. The food is still warm but not for long. I guess some other people here, that German couple, have chickens. They give eggs to people on a rotation. We won the jackpot today as a welcome gift. So it's scrambled eggs today."

"Really?" Kurt said, in a shock.

"I know, right? Come on, let's eat."

Tyler and Kurt voraciously ate the plates of eggs.

Tyler looked up from his nearly clean plate. Just a single piece of egg remained. "Kurt, I want to stay here. I think it's a safe place. There are more people. Winter is starting to come. I think it's a good call."

Kurt felt himself getting nervous. "The only reason we are alive is because we have kept moving. We can't just stop now."

"Kurt, we have been running from an unknown existence. Here we have a village, we have protection, we have fresh water, we have propane and gas. This place is perfect."

"I still feel in my gut, we need to keep moving. Stay on the run."

"I know you are holding onto your dream of seeing your brother again, but this place changes everything."

"This isn't about my brother."

"Of course it is."

Kurt couldn't lie. "It isn't only about him."

Tyler shook his head.

"Listen, I'm telling you, if we want to be really safe, we need to keep moving. If we become stagnant, something bad is going to happen. I feel it in my gut."

"Look around you, Kurt!" Tyler gestured with his hands in a wide circle. "The world is gone. Here we can have a sense of normal."

Kurt asked, extremely confused, "Are you saying you want to stay here permanently?"

"This is a fresh start. After everything, this place could be a new home, for all of us."

"I can't do that. You know I have to get back home."

"This can be home."

"I can't."

Tyler leaned forward, lowering his tone. "Then let's stay here for a couple of months. For winter at least. If you still feel the same after that time, then we can talk about us all going together. I don't want to try roughing it in the winter, man. That's just not smart. You have to see that."

Kurt mulled it over. Winter snowstorms would be coming soon. The rain and freeze earlier had made the roads hell. Full winter would be impassable. "You may be right," he said.

"I am."

"Fine. Let's stay until spring," Kurt said, nodding his head.

"Deal," Tyler said, smiling.

The Settlement: Outbreak Day +42

Kurt zipped his jacket up higher, attempting to fight against the cold. The Russian freeze had come in completely. Ice and snow had covered the whole forest. He was walking back to the settlement after Tyler had just relieved him of guard duty.

Guard duty had been split into shorter times during the winter. Philip, Brandon, Jonathan, Kurt, Tyler and three other men in the camp each had solo guard duties lasting only three hours, each on a set rotation, to minimize the time spent sitting in the cold. To make things worse, the mini heater had stopped working. The tree blind was now an icebox.

As Kurt arrived home, he welcomed the warmth of the RV as he opened the door and a wave of heat hit him. He sat down and took his boots and frozen coat off, feeling himself come back to life.

"Welcome back!" Liz said in a peppy tone.

"Wow, you're happy! How was your shift?" Kurt asked as he melted and put on a large sweater.

"It was good! I got done a little early today. I guess people aren't using as much water since it's cold." Water purification had been set on a similar rotation. Liz was on the same hours shift as Kurt. "It felt extra cold today though. Thankfully since we spend a fair amount of time carrying stuff around, once you get moving, it sort of doesn't affect you as much."

"Lucky. I froze my ass off just sitting there staring at nothing."

"No, not that cute little butt," Liz said, laughing and winking at Kurt. "Hey, do you want to play cards again?"

"Sure, what's the game today? Poker again? I smoked you last time we played that!"

"Yeah, you did! Thank God we were just playing for play chips and not something more serious. Today's game is cribbage. Do you know how to play?"

"Yeah, cribbage is pretty fun. Do we have a board?"

"No, I figured we'd just count up to 121."

"Oh, gotcha. Cool, let's play."

"I think I'll beat you today. I'm feeling lucky."

"Really?" Kurt said sarcastically while moving to the table. "I wouldn't bet on it if I were you."

"Oh? Do you want to make a bet?" Liz responded. "We could make this really interesting."

Kurt felt his heart skip a beat for a second. His intuition told him he could push it and rekindle what had sparked that night in the back of the RV. "You feel that lucky, huh?"

"Yeah," Liz smiled at Kurt sitting on the other side of the table. "What kind of bet are you thinking?"

Kurt had ideas in his mind, none that would end up good. He listened to his heart. "No bets today, just the right to know I beat you in the game of your choosing."

"Lame," Liz said back, smirking.

"Shuffle."

"Fine." Liz shuffled the cards and started playing. She started talking in the middle of the play round. "Eight, oh, so guess what."

"Eighteen for two. What?"

"Twenty-eight. I know someone who has a crush on you."

"Go. Who?" Kurt was afraid that she was going to say herself. He also secretly wanted her to say that.

"Thirty-one for two. Brigiette, the Austrian girl."

"Four. Really? I've talked to her like five times."

"Well she does. Thirteen."

"Probably just a matter of me being the only guy her age around here. Not like there's a lot of choice. Twenty-three."

"Kurt, any girl would be lucky to have you. You're cute. You're funny. You're kind. You're a good kisser."

Kurt looked at Liz with a guilty face.

"Sorry, but it's true." Liz put her cards down on the table, suddenly looking sad.

"What's wrong?" Kurt asked.

"That's how I used to describe Tyler. Key word, *used to*."

"That's two words," Kurt quipped jokingly.

Liz wasn't amused. "Seriously, I thought things would get better now that we're safe. They haven't. I just don't know what to do. I just want to be happy again. Happy like I am when it's just me and you."

"Give him time. It's hard to be open emotionally, period. Even more so in a zombie apocalypse."

"I know it is, but all the things I loved about him are disappearing. He may as well be a zombie. It's killing off the best parts of him. It's not doing that to you. You're still your amazing self."

"Thanks, but that's a little exaggeration. I wouldn't say I'm amazing. I'm a lazy kid who just happened to survive because people around me saved me."

"That's not true, not even a little bit, Kurt." They both sat quiet for a second. Liz broke the silence. "Can I ask you a favor? Talk to him. Try getting him to have fun. Just smile again and lighten up. Please."

"Okay."

"Thanks, and in the meantime, talk to that girl Brigiette more."

"No promises there."

"Kurt."

"How many points do you have in your hand?"

"Seriously, Kurt."

"Look, if you win this game, I'll go talk to her. If I win, I don't force social interaction, deal?"

"Deal." Liz picked her cards up. "I'm going to kick your ass this game."

The Settlement: Outbreak Day +49

Palm trees waved in the breeze, their green leaves shining brightly in the midday sun that was beating down on South Beach. Joe and Kurt stood in swimsuits, tan from the amount of time they had spent playing catch with a football over their summer break. It had been the last week before Joe started high school. A beautiful moment frozen in time.

Frozen was exactly what Kurt was now. He sat against the back of the icy hunting blind. He was supposed to be looking out on the horizon, but instead he was focused on the picture he had found in the bottom of his pack. That summer had been an amazing time. He was now staring at Joe's smile, committing it to his memory. Kurt glanced around the blind. All of his things were strewn across the floor. He had gotten so bored that he had decided to empty and pack his pack again. Before finding the picture, Kurt had been most surprised by how many needles he had pulled out of the bag. Most had stuck to his sleeping bag and lean-to from his first night camping in the wilderness.

Kurt probably needed to repack his pack soon, but looking at frozen pine trees, he had no motivation. This place was cold, hard and unforgiving. Kurt looked back at the photo. It was the opposite. Kurt could almost feel the soft sand, the warm sun and his brother's arm around him. A tear crawled its way out of his eye.

Kurt sniffled and looked at the setting sun. "Dear Lord, thank you for saving me and bringing me to a place where I'm safe. Lord, please, wherever Joe is right now, send your angels to him. Keep him safe. Amen."

Florida Keys: Outbreak Day +52

The wind blast from the helicopter blades froze Joe's face as he sat in the back of the chopper.

"There is the smoke, sir!" Joe heard over the wind on his headphones.

Joe leaned out the side of the chopper, the wind blast intensifying. He spotted white smoke rising from a small Key in the middle of nowhere. They were miles away from the main strip of islands that made up the Florida Keys. "Take us over it."

The pilot flew them over the small island. Joe could see a large bonfire burning in the center. As they flew to the far end, he saw three people waving, two adults and one child, standing on a long dock with a sunken boat at the end.

"Martinell." Joe turned to look at the man sitting across from him, the other member of his fire team that was with him on this rescue mission. "You and I are going down to secure the passengers. Once we have them secure, we'll radio up." Joe pointed at the other man in the rear part of the helicopter, a search and rescue wench operator. "You'll lower the cable."

The man spoke back over the radio. "Hook each of them up one at a time. Let them know we'll swing out of the water first to make sure we don't turn them into a human wrecking ball and take y'all out."

Joe nodded. "Roger."

The pilot joined the conversation on the headset. "Captain Feller, I'm going to drop you on that dock using the ropes. Then I'll move to a higher-elevation hovering point to avoid wind blast as best as possible."

"Roger. Martinell, hook up the rope on the other side."

Both men hooked up two black ropes, each about twenty feet in length. The pilot hovered over the end of the dock as they threw the ropes out and slid down to the dock's decking. They each threw their rope off the end of the dock, ensuring they didn't snag, as the helicopter climbed higher. As the wind blast and noise dissipated, the three people ran up to them. It was a woman in her thirties, a man a few years older and a young girl.

"Are you all okay?" Martinell asked as they approached.

"Thank you so much," the man said. "We weren't sure what to do."

"How did you get out here?" Martinell asked.

"We own this island. My wife, my daughter and I were camping. We heard over the radio what was happening, so we decided to stay here as long as we could, fishing to stay alive. Then disaster struck. During that last storm, our boat hit the dock and damaged the hull, sinking it. There aren't any good fish around here, so we didn't know where we were going to get food next. A signal fire was all I could think of." The man, woman and girl all had tears running down their faces.

"That was a rough storm. Several boats were sunk in Key West," Joe said. He thought to himself, *thank God Kira and the girls got through unscathed.* "Anyone else here?"

"No. Just us three."

"Okay, here's what's going to happen. We have three harnesses. Martinell will help you get them on. That helicopter will come and lower a rope with a hook attached to a wench. One at a time, we'll raise you up. It's important that you stay calm. It's okay to grab the cable, just try not to flail around. The pilot is going to take you over the water first and then bring you up. Simple as that. Got it?"

They all nodded.

After a few minutes, they all had their harnesses on. A few minutes later, the last member of the trapped family was ascending into the air. "Amazing to see a family together in all this. Do you have family alive, sir?" Martinell asked Joe.

"Yes, and I don't know. I have a girl I traveled down here with and some kids I rescued in Key West, so they are pretty much family to me now. And I have a brother somewhere in Russia, plus our parents are on a cruise ship called the *Aleutian Dream* in Alaska. I'm not sure about them. I hope they're all alive and somewhere this whole shit show is far away from. What about you, Martinell?"

"No parents or anyone in Key West. I have a brother who was in New York, but I haven't heard from him. The comm. guys are making more and more contact with people around the country and the world, so maybe we'll be able to find both our brothers soon."

The cable was on its way back down. "You're up, Martinell."

Martinell grabbed the hook and clipped it into his harness. He waved to the helicopter, and he swung over the water. Joe watched as Martinell was pulled into the belly of the chopper.

Soon Joe was being pulled up himself. He spun as the cable pulled him into the air. The spin paused as he was looking at the island, still on fire. Joe stared at the flames, thinking about what Martinell had said. *Maybe I'll find you soon, brother. I hope you're still out there, Kurt.*

The Settlement: Outbreak Day +57

The orange flames of the bonfire licked into the starlit sky. The occasional pop of a pinecone sent sparks into the blackness.

It was another Friday night and another end-of-the-week celebration. Although, most of the camp hadn't come out for tonight's much smaller fire. Winter would soon be coming to a close, but the cold was holding on with all its might. Only a few intrepid fire revelers had made it out tonight.

Kurt and Liz sat, sharing a log and a blanket, and squeezed closely together to share body heat and fight back the freeze. One older grandma-and-grandpa type sat in lawn chairs close to the fire, holding each other's thick-mitten-wrapped hands. A few kids roasted marshmallows with their mom while their dad stood farther away from the fire, chain-smoking a cigarette, each puff looking like a desperate attempt to suck the life out of the cigarette as fast as possible and return to the warmth of the RV.

There was no dancing tonight. All the musicians and party animals had stayed home. It was just too cold. Everyone just sat quietly, watching the fire, enjoying the sight and trying to absorb some of its heat.

Kurt's watch beeped and shined a green Indiglo hue.

"Is it your shift already?" Liz asked.

"No, not yet. I've still got an hour until I go relieve Tyler. But I'm going to head back to the RV and get as warm as possible before guard duty," Kurt said.

"I'll come with you," Liz said as they both stood up and she wrapped the blanket around herself.

They each gave a few goodbye waves to everyone. Everyone nodded except the man smoking. He simply glared. Kurt could sense some judgment, or maybe he was judging himself. Liz had become very important to him. He definitely had feelings for her, feelings he felt were inappropriate. He didn't voice them or act on them. They were just good friends. As long as it stayed that way, it was okay, even if he didn't want it to stay that way.

After a short shuffling hike with frozen joints, Kurt held the RV open for Liz to go inside, and he followed. The warmth welcomed him. "Oh yeah. That's awesome."

"It's so much warmer in here," Liz said, shedding the blanket and throwing it down on the couch. "The fire barely held back the cold tonight. I still loved it though. But I wish the whole camp still came out. I miss the fun of it all. When we first got here, there was so much enjoyment, and music, and dancing."

"Yeah, you used to have so much fun dancing!" Kurt said with a smile on his face.

"Dancing is something so special to me. It's just when I can completely let go. Or at least I used to. The last time I danced was at a bonfire a few weeks ago. Tyler and I went. But when I was dancing, he just sat there. I could feel his judging stare. It ruined it. He used to dance with me. Now he's just cold, and it's stealing my happiness."

Kurt sat quietly, unsure of what to say or do. Then inspiration hit. Kurt started drumming the table and beatboxing, poorly. He then started to dance even worse while singing/beatboxing/humming his favorite song from Miami Beach, "Danza Kuduro." Kurt had heard it a thousand times blasting out from beach clubs.

Liz laughed, a giant smile spreading across her face.

"Come on!" Kurt said.

Liz jumped over and started dancing with Kurt. They danced for a few minutes, until Kurt lost track of the song and his breath. They both sat down on the couch, laughing, as the music "stopped."

"Thanks, Kurt, I needed that," Liz said. She turned and gave Kurt a big hug. "Thanks for being such an amazing guy and friend."

"You're welcome." Kurt held her close, cherishing this moment. No matter what happened in the future, Kurt knew he would remember this moment.

"How about another dance?" Liz whispered into his ear.

"Absolutely," Kurt said.

Liz hopped up and started singing "Get Low." Kurt started laughing so hard he could barely breathe.

Yet he found the energy to hop up and join Liz on the dance floor.

Kurt walked to guard duty that night with a smile on his face, warmth in his body, and a beat in his ears.

The Settlement: Outbreak Day +65

The days were starting to warm up. The icy hold of the Russian winter was starting to subside. Along with the sun came the return of the old-style shifts at the gate. Kurt and Tyler had long shifts together again. After the winter solitude, it was a strange and welcome thing to have someone to talk to.

Kurt and Tyler had started playing cards for a fun, competitive way to pass shifts. A deck of playing cards was one of the better finds from Kurt's never-not-there backpacking kit over the winter. So now one of them would play a game of solitaire using Vegas rules while the other watched the horizon. Loser of that night's shift had to do the dishes and clean the RV after dinner. The melting snow had started to turn the ground to mud, meaning there was a lot of cleaning to do.

"Damn! Negative five points," Kurt said as he ran out of plays.

Tyler laughed as they traded places. "You're going to be maid tonight for sure."

"Yeah," Kurt said as he shifted on the hunting stool to see out better. "It's bonfire night tonight too."

"Guess you're going to be late." Tyler jabbed playfully as he shuffled the deck of cards.

"Yeah."

"Well on the bright side, maybe by that time, the girls will be dancing," Tyler said, starting to lay the cards out for his turn.

"True that. God bless the climate getting warmer. A few minutes of dancing to the guitar music from that Russian guy and layers will be coming off."

Tyler asked Kurt, "Any particular girls you want to see the layers come off of?"

Kurt laughed out the window. "Well I know that girl Brigiette wants to see my layers come off."

"Yeah?"

"Ha ha ha, yeah. Liz told me a while ago, and lately that girl has been pretty upfront about looking at me."

"She's not here with someone, right?" Tyler asked, suddenly more interested in the conversation than the card game he had started.

"No, she's definitely single."

"Then why don't you?"

"Let her take my layers off?"

"And return the favor."

"Nah, man."

"Oh come on, man! Why not? Someone else stole your heart? Do you have a secret girl waiting for you back home?"

Kurt laughed. "No, nothing like that."

"What then? Just a pussy?"

"Thanks."

"Just saying. Why wouldn't you at least see what happens?"

"Well it's getting warmer now."

"Yeah, I noticed, so what? You think she'll only like you when it's colder than the devil's ballsack?"

Kurt laughed. "Well we're going to be leaving soon. I don't want to be entangled or get attached here right now."

"Leaving?" Tyler said, confused.

"Yeah." Kurt turned so he was facing Tyler. "That was the deal."

"The deal was to stay here and see how it went. Then talk about it. Well it's going pretty well. I don't want to leave," Tyler said, defensively.

"What? Are you serious?" Kurt nearly shouted at him.

Tyler looked at him, standing his ground. "Yeah, I really am. We're safe here. We should stay. We can have a life here. I was talking to Philip the other day, and he is talking about farming in a few months, cutting down some trees and building actual houses. It's actual rebuilding."

"Tyler, don't do this."

"Do what?"

"I can't stay here, you know that. I have to get back to my brother," Kurt said.

Tyler jumped in. "And eventually you might, but for now, we need to rebuild."

Kurt's stomach churned. His intuition shouted, screamed and revolted: *RUN.* "Tyler, you and Liz have become something that mean a lot to me. I don't want to leave without you, but I will if I have to."

"You're seriously going to leave?"

"I have to. Look, the truth is, this mission of finding my brother, it's more than just a dream, or a desire. It's my reason for life at this point. I have to follow it."

"Look, I've been making good progress with this satellite phone." Tyler pulled the previously left-for-dead phone out of his coat pocket. "I started looking at it again. I found a way to make it dial properly. All I have to do is find a powerful enough antenna and we can get a call out. Give me a chance to get a call out and you can call your bro. If he answers, we'll all go. If not, we'll stay. How does that sound?"

"I don't know. I just have to—" Kurt was interrupted by another voice.

"Hey, you two up there?" Brandon called out.

Kurt peeked out the window of the blind. "Yeah."

"We can come back later if you want to finish jacking each other off," Jonathan said.

"On our way down," Kurt said back.

"Look, Kurt, let's go back to the RV, and we can talk about this more, okay?"

"I can't stay."

"Can we talk about this more at the RV?"

"Sure. I really do want Liz and you to come with me."

"Okay, let's talk about it more."

Tyler and Kurt packed up and slid down the ladder. As they passed Brandon and Jonathan, Jonathan said, "Enjoy the bonfire, guys. Next week we're trading shifts so we can have some fun! I'm tired of missing every bonfire."

"That might not be a problem," Kurt murmured.

"What?" Brandon asked.

"Don't worry about it," Tyler said.

Jonathan ran to the ladder. "Dibs on the warm side."

Brandon turned to give chase. "Oh hell no!"

Walking back to the settlement was not a fun experience, thanks to the wet, sopping landscape. The tundra would refreeze, but for now, everything was dripping in melted snow.

"This mud sucks," Tyler said, nearly falling as his foot slid.

"No joke," Kurt said as he sloshed through the mud. "Sure you want to stay here?"

"Shut up," Tyler said back.

"Thank God I have massive, size-twelve feet," Kurt said.

"Oh yeah, and my size nines are baby feet," Tyler said sourly. His next step proved his point. As he planted his boot, it sank deeply into the ground. "Mother!"

Kurt laughed. "Here, grab my hand." He helped Tyler pull himself out of the hole. As his boot pulled free, a strange milky-white steam came up. "What's that from?" Kurt asked.

Tyler was busy trying to clean the muck off his boot that now felt like it weighed one hundred pounds. "I don't know."

"Weird. Maybe you have nasty feet." Kurt laughed.

"Very funny. If that were the case, the rest of the ground wouldn't be steaming too."

"What?" Kurt asked, still staring at the hole. "Well look."

Kurt looked around. The same milky-white steam was coming from the ground all over. The settlement itself was covered by a small fog from the steam.

"What the hell is that?"

Tyler was just as surprised. "I don't know. Maybe it's just something that happens out here."

Kurt didn't think so. "Really?"

"Let's go find Philip and figure out what's happening." Tyler's voice gave away his nerves.

Kurt and Tyler took off toward Philip's RV. Liz saw their faces as they passed her on their way to Philip's.

"What's going on?" Liz asked.

"What are you doing out here?" Tyler asked.

"It's my turn on the water pump. Where are y'all headed in such a hurry?"

"We're looking for Philip," Kurt said as he kept moving toward Philip's RV.

"He's by the fire pit with his truck," Liz said.

"Come with us," Kurt said.

The three of them found Philip standing by the back of his truck.

Philip turned, saw their looks. "What's wrong?"

Kurt said, fairly frantic, "The ground is steaming!"

Philip looked at them with a quizzical look on his face. "It's just fog, Kurt."

Kurt shot back, a little frazzled still, "This isn't fog. Look, it's coming from the ground."

"That's what fog does. I'm sure you're not used to the woods, so I can understand the confusion."

"It's the afternoon. Since when does fog start in the afternoon?"

"It can happen, Kurt. Just relax," Philip said.

"Look around you. Something is wrong," Kurt pleaded. "My gut is telling me zombies are coming."

Tyler joined the conversation, trying to calm Kurt down. "Maybe it is just fog, man."

Philip jumped in. "Yes, it is. We are perfectly safe here. Kurt, how many zombies have you seen since you've been here?"

Kurt answered, "None, but still—"

"Still what, Kurt?" Philip didn't let him finish.

"I feel like something is wrong. We've been here too long. We need to keep moving."

"What are you talking about?" Philip asked.

"My intuition is telling me that we need to get out of here. It's telling me that we are in danger."

"Your intuition? Are you serious?" Philip was not amused.

"Yes!" Kurt yelled.

"Kurt, you need to calm down. I don't know what is wrong with you, but this place is safe." Philip's face began turning red. "There is nothing wrong! Look around you! Look at all the people we have saved, who currently call this place home. Look at how safe they are!"

"Something is wrong!" Kurt screamed.

"Keep your voice down," Tyler said. "You're going to cause a scene."

"A scene? I'm trying to tell you—" Kurt was cut off by Philip, now angry.

"I know what you're trying to say, and you need to stop. This place is safe. This is my new home. This is where my boys are protected. This is where you are protected. Only an act of God can change that!"

Instead came an act of hell.

A bony hand shot up out of the ground and grabbed Philip's left leg around the calf. With a tearing sound, the hand pulled his foot and leg into the ground. Philip let out a huge scream as a crunch echoed from under the dirt. His face was full of fear and pain.

Tyler and Kurt grabbed his arms and pulled with all their strength. Liz joined them. Their three grunts joined Philip's painful screams in a terrible symphony. Their efforts paid off. With a final pull,

Philip came free, sending all four of them falling to the ground.

Where Philip's lower leg used to be was now a bloody mess. The leg had stringy, torn skin dangling loose while blood poured out. Tendons, muscle fiber and blood vessels were easily visible through gaping wounds.

Philip's face turned white as the blood quickly drained from his body. Philip tried to grab at his leg, screaming into the sky.

"Hold him!" Kurt yelled at Tyler and Liz as he tried to put pressure on the wound with his hands, trying to stop the gushing blood. Tyler and Liz held Philip down while holding his hands. He was writhing in pain. "Tyler, give me your belt!" Kurt yelled.

Tyler reached to grab his buckle and remove the belt. As he did, another hand reached for him. A diseased hand shot up from the ground below, wildly grabbing at the air. Tyler fell back and scooted away. "What the fuck!" He grabbed the pistol he kept in his waistband and fired several shots into the ground.

As an answer to the shots, the ground all around them began to echo with a new sound: clawing and scraping, like fingernails scraping against a chalkboard. Hands were clawing against buried wood and rock. The sound sent a chill through Kurt's body. He had always hated that sound. Now he was surrounded by it. It infiltrated every part of the camp and echoed through the tree around them. Hands started popping up through the dirt all across the camp. It looked like a terrible version of a whack-amole game. Undead arms and heads began springing from the dirt. They were everywhere. A hand shot up right between Kurt's legs. He rolled to the side, escaping its reach. Kurt grabbed Philip's handgun from its holster and pointed it at the waving, wriggling hand.

"Tyler!" Liz screamed. Right behind Tyler's left foot, a zombie head popped out of the ground, its gnashing jaws just a few inches from Tyler's heel.

Tyler spun around and fired a round straight through the zombie's skull. It exploded.

Another zombie popped up in the gap between Kurt and Philip. Another started to crawl out of the ground separating Liz and Tyler from Kurt. Kurt and Liz connected stares. "Run!" Kurt screamed. "Meet at the RV!"

Kurt pushed himself backward, away from Philip and the zombie, turned and started running. He had the longer path to the RV, so he would have to run in a roundabout path. Kurt pulled hard on his backpack straps to seal it to his body as best as possible. The zombie that had separated him from Liz and Tyler pulled himself free from the ground and gave chase. Kurt took off, attempting to run around the tankers and then come back around to the RV.

Tyler fired a round, killing a zombie that had half-excavated himself. "Let's go, Liz!"

"What about Philip?" Liz was still holding Philip's hand.

Tyler took a quick glance at the now-unconscious man and shot him in the face. "Run!" Liz was frozen in shock at watching Philip's face explode in front of her. Tyler grabbed her. "Come on!"

People were screaming, and undead assailants were everywhere. Their "safe" little village was now a hunting ground. It quickly became a game of deadly dodgeball. Kurt was doing well on his sprint for the tankers but couldn't lose his focus. He turned to see how close the zombie chasing him was. In that split second, another zombie came around the side of the tanker Kurt was close to. Kurt tried to stop in his tracks, but the wet ground gave way. He slide tackled right between the zombie's legs and right underneath the tanker. Kurt crawled frantically until he came up on the other side. He kept running. As he looked toward the RV parking area, now across the road, he saw the RV where Brigiette lived. It was rocking, and a bloody hand shot up onto the window. He paused for a second, thinking. "Shit," Kurt cursed. He knew what he should do, but he didn't want to. His pursuer came down the road. Its white, milky eyes hungered for Kurt. Kurt took off into the forest, leaving everyone else behind. The zombie was fast on his heels. It was up to Kurt's running ability yet again.

Florida Keys: Outbreak Day +45

A slight chill ran through Kira as the late winter attempted to hold onto its cool. The morning air blew in from the south, carrying the scent of ocean loam.

Kira was sitting in the gently rocking fishing boat, breathing in a deep breath of relaxation. Out here on the ocean was one of the greatest feelings in the world. She had gone to Miami Beach for the water. Sun-drenched days on a boat were all she had ever dreamed of. Growing up in a small town in Iowa, she had endured biting winters and sleet-consumed fall days. She had moved to the Sunshine State knowing no one and not having much money. It was a leap of faith, a step toward her dream. Since her mom had died, she had always wanted to escape. She was strong for her sister and their dad, but she had formed a desire. Kira wanted to live a different life, be a different person. She desperately desired freedom from the pressures of being strong. She had wanted to just be whoever she felt like. There wouldn't be someone relying on her or telling her what was right or wrong. Kira wanted no real responsibilities, just to be free.

A smile spread across her face. Fate, it seemed, had other plans. She was now a parent. Kira was a surrogate mother for Christine, Elizabeth and Jack. Now it wasn't just about her survival but theirs too. It was a lot of pressure.

Taking care of three small children was hard. It was taking its toll on Kira. Her fishing trips had slowly started to become longer and longer. Out here, there were no worries, no responsibilities and no fears. What if she did something wrong? Up to this point, she was trying her best. When in doubt, she would ask herself, "What would Mom have done?" It had worked so far. But what if she couldn't be the mom these kids needed?

It was all so much to bear. How do you take care of, console and discipline three small children who have lost their father, don't know what happened to their mother and are stuck living on a boat a million miles away from home, all in the middle of the zombie apocalypse? She was only twenty-two years old, at least for a few more hours. At 11:00 a.m., Kira would be twenty-three.

Today was Kira's birthday. Growing up, birthdays hadn't been a super-huge tradition, for Kira at least. Winter birthdays were less fun when the weather was cold enough to kill. Her sister's summer birthday parties were always major events. They went to water parks, had group picnics with bonfires, had fun at Six Flags or had some other crazy adventure. Kira's were usually at some indoor place that was just anywhere warm. She hadn't told Joe or the kids that today was her birthday. With everything going on the last few months, the kids adjusting to not having their dad, constantly asking when they would see him again, and Joe gone so much with the military, it didn't feel like a time to celebrate. So instead she had decided to have a celebration on her own. Her gift to herself was an extra ten minutes on the water this morning. Sitting there, not fishing, just relaxing. Just letting the world drift away for a little bit. No thoughts of anything specific allowed, just feeling the moment.

Kira's mind began to wander to memories of her past. She thought about happy childhood memories. Kira felt the warmth of a hug from her mother. The joy and carefree feeling of partying on the beach with her friends in Miami. She thought of her dad and sister setting up the Monopoly board as a Christmas tradition. She would never see them again. She would never hear their voices. She thought about them more deeply. Could she still see their faces?

What about Joe? Could she his face? Yes. Kira could recall every pockmark, every curve and dimple in his face. Was he okay? A feeling of longing overwhelmed her, and she began to cry. It had been weeks since she had seen or even heard from him. Not knowing if he was going to come back was torture. She needed his help with the kids, but that wasn't all. There was something else, something that had been growing since he rescued her from that office in Miami Beach.

At first, Kira had denied it. She assumed it had to be the result of a false sense of attraction that only came from his saving her. It had to be. Weeks had passed, and that little spark in her heart hadn't died out; it had flared. The shock of what happened had worn off. Still, she felt a longing to feel his arms around her. Kira felt stupid. She hadn't even hugged the guy. She needed to grow up and become more than she was. She had people who relied on her now. None of what she told herself mattered. There was something real in her feelings for him. She began to dream of Joe as the gentle waves rocked the boat. Kira allowed herself to slip into a waking dream.

She saw him walking down the row of ships. Kira ran out the back, bounding to him. He caught her with his arms open wide, spinning her in a big circle. He pulled her close and stared into her eyes. She leaned closer as the distance between their lips lessened, until . . .

BEEP, BEEP, BEEP

Her dream came crashing down around her. The Casio on her wrist had brought Kira back to reality a half-second too soon. The fishing trip was over. It was time to return to normal life. The birthday-trip bonus time was over. Kira reeled in her lines that still lay baited in the water. Looking at her catch, she was proud. Today had been a great day. The ship was filled with three quotas' worth of fish. Today she would get a good amount of fuel and extra barter.

Kira opened the notebook she had taken from Hank and checked the spot she had fished today off the list. She was careful to keep a random rotation to the list. Overfishing one area would drain it of its catch, and establishing too steady a pattern could teach the fish to avoid her. Putting the notebook carefully away in her front jeans pocket, Kira turned the boat on and steered back toward Key West.

Kira pulled into the Key West Marina around 11:00 a.m. After getting her fuel allotments and turning in one of her catch baskets, she sailed around the cove to a long, makeshift pier. It had been built to barter and sell fish and fishing supplies. Kira piloted the small boat to a yellow canopy and tied up. A large woman edged up to the side of the dock. She wore bright-yellow flip-flops, a bright-yellow sundress and an ivory thatch hat. At almost 300 pounds, she was a massive figure.

"Hello, dearie! How was this morning?" The woman looked down at the catch in Kira's boat.

"It was great, Frannie!" Kira lifted the first of the two quota baskets onto the pier.

Frannie leaned closer over the basket, inspecting the fish. Kira hefted the second basket up next to the first. Frannie wiggled her nose.

"They look smaller than usual, my dear."

Kira wasn't buying it. "Nice try, Frannie. The usual price sound fair?"

Frannie smiled yes.

Kira dealt with Frannie because she was consistent. Kira may have been able to haggle for more with other vendors, but after time, they would want to get better deals or favors. Frannie was straightforward. That was worth a little less profit. Frannie shuffled, shifting her weight side to side and opened up a locked trunk. She pulled out some fishing line, hooks, lures and a rare power-bait pack. Frannie handed them to Kira, who in turn, examined each one. Kira nodded approvingly.

Next Frannie gave Kira a bar of soap and a stack of gold coins. Gold had become the currency accepted by all the vendors. Kira hopped down into her boat.

"How do you keep bringing in this kind of catch?" Frannie asked.

"Maybe it's just because I'm that good." Kira smiled at Frannie.

"Oh, dear, I'm not complaining, but no one is that good." Frannie tilted her head down, looking through cocked eyes at Kira.

"I guess I am."

"Mm-hmm." Frannie wasn't buying it.

"I just know all the spots."

"How?"

Kira smirked. She pulled the notebook out of her pocket and waved it. "I have a secret weapon."

Frannie laughed, reeling back on her heels as a smile spread across her face. "Dearie! You are full of surprises."

Kira answered with a shrug of her shoulders. She revved the engine. "See you tomorrow, Frannie." And she steered toward the Marquis, heading home with her bounty in hand.

The dark shadows consumed him. His roost was well thought out and picked. He watched Kira closely from under a sea-worn wood overhang. His eyes tracked her as she sailed away from the market dock. Smoke slid out of his mouth from a hand-rolled cigar. It billowed and curved around his nose and slid around the bill of his cap.

He had had too many catchless days. Now this little girl had found something. Something he needed.

The red notebook burned through his retinas. Now he only needed the right moment. Soon that notebook and the knowledge of those secret spots would be his. Nothing would stand in the way of Chester Almont. It was time to start implementing his scheme. A sickly smile crept across his lips as he slinked away down the dock.

Florida Keys: Outbreak Day +62

Joe sat up from his metal bed. He had fallen asleep on the bench inside the helicopter. Over the last three weeks, his fire squad had been engaged in so many missions that he couldn't keep track anymore.

The fight for land had been steady. Executing the plan and saving the random stranded person was working, but he had gotten little to no rest. A few weeks earlier, a distress call had come from the main oil rig that supplied fuel for the military. Someone had taken Enerjax by accident, mistaking it for Advil. Everyone had died before the two fire teams arrived. The fire teams themselves lost a few men clearing the platform. Joe's team had been on their mandatory rest at the time, so his men were saved, but he still felt the losses. One fire team had to stay on the rig to operate it with a few men transferred from another rig. The commander had suspended the required break policy to keep up with the same need with fewer men. Joe was tired.

His boots hit the floor of the chopper with a loud clang as he swung himself to a sitting position. Joe rubbed his face with his hands, attempting to rub some feeling back into his skin. He rolled his head from side to side, cracking joints and releasing a kink that had settled into his upper back. He looked at his all-black G-Shock watch. It had been a gift from his brother a few years ago. The timepiece was his good luck charm. As long as he wore the watch, he felt invincible. He felt his brother's love. *I hope you're still out there, Kurt.*

At 07:34, it was time to move. With a large exertion of energy, Joe climbed off the bench and out of the helicopter. The briefing for this morning was scheduled to begin at 08:00. His team was leading the first mop-up of the next Key on their way up the chain of islands.

"Hey, Captain." Martinell walked up, sounding concerned.

"Yeah, I'm coming," Joe said, shaking the last cobwebs from his head.

"What? Oh, the brief. Yeah, you got a few minutes. But uh, uh, I have to tell you something. Well . . ." Martinell was having trouble talking.

"Spit it out, man, it's too early."

"Okay." Martinell took a big breath, gathering himself. "You said your parents were on the *Aleutian Dream*, right?"

"Yeah," Joe answered.

"Well I heard from the comm. guys who are in communication with a Coast Guard unit in Alaska. They had news of your mom and dad's cruise ship."

"Well?" Joe asked.

"Apparently the Coast Guard found it floating at sea, and well, it was something terrible. I'm sorry, man."

Joe felt his stomach drop. "Thanks."

"Yeah, I thought you should hear from someone you know. I'll see you in the brief."

Don't think about it now. Save that shit, Joe thought to himself, steeling his nerves for what he had to do next. Joe became a rock. He walked into the briefing room and sat down on a hard chair. It matched his countenance. There were still a few minutes until the brief. Joe felt for the first time how much he didn't want to be there. He had heard this same thing so many times. It was the same plan. He could restate it from memory at this point. It hadn't changed. It didn't need too. It was working. The only thing that changed was the name of the stupid island they moved on to. Joe didn't even know what Florida Key they were up to at this point. They weren't even Keys anymore, just mixes of palm trees, bloody sand and screaming zombies. Joe's last few weeks had been a blurry horror show.

They were only animals. The zombies were controlled only by their natural instincts, simple creatures of hunger and habit. Compared to Joe's trained and now battle-hardened fire team, it wasn't even fair. Joe's team had never lost a man and had sent hundreds of the undead back to the full-dead stage. Today would be no different.

Joe began to daydream of the soft bed on the Marquis yacht harbored just a few miles away. Joe hadn't been back since New Year's. There hadn't been time. He could picture Kira and the children. He hoped they were doing well and had stayed safe. They were his responsibility. He had pulled them all out of the mayhem of South Beach. Now he didn't even know if they were okay. Did they have enough fuel or enough food? Joe felt a twinge of guilt spike through his body. Was what he was doing worth it? The missions were slowly regaining and clawing back piece by piece a world that didn't exist anymore. What would they find when they reached the mainland? Was it worth it?

"Attention on deck!"

Joe was jolted from his depressed chain of thought and stood at attention. The Navy insisted on using ship vernacular even though the ready room was inside a building on land.

Commander Church, the officer in charge of organizing the island-hopping maneuvers, stood at the front of the room, behind a folding table.

"At ease. Good morning, everyone. We've all been here before, so I won't be overly descriptive. Today's mission is to secure the opposite side of this bridge."

The commander pushed a button, and a satellite image came up on a projector screen behind him. The image showed a bridge that had a small section missing from the center. The Navy had destroyed it with C4 explosives. On one side of the burned-out bridge was the smoking remains of the target island. A black cloud obstructed most of the view.

"As you can see, the terrain is a little different than before. There are no mangrove swamps near the shore here. One side of the road is covered in palm trees, and the other is plain, flat ground, a fill-in for a residential development that didn't get a chance to happen. Unfortunately it appears the bombing runs hit an underground tank of oil. This black smoke is the burning residue of that oil. It should clear before you arrive. We are currently bombing the bridge on the other side of the island, sealing it off. Once the fire teams have secured the other side, our engineers will be bridging across, followed by ground troops." The image on the screen went blank, and the commander took his place in the center of the room. "Combatant levels are estimated to be minimal, but be careful. We have been receiving strange reports from the lookouts on the ships."

A young sergeant echoed from the back of the small room. "What kind of reports?"

"Apparently the zombies have been attacking trees, and they are reporting dust mixed in with the smoke. That's all they could say."

Joe chuckled.

The commander asked Joe, "Is something funny?"

Joe's cockiness showed openly. "They're attacking trees now. How dumb can zombies be?"

The whole room shared his sentiment, laughing all around. The commander sported a smile himself.

"Okay, okay, that's enough, everyone. Are there any questions?

"Are we going to have any air support?

"Yes, the Black Hawks will have fire authority after dropping their teams off."

The room was silent except the noise of a soldier adjusting his seat in the metal chair. They had all run this mission already. It was simple at this point.

"Everyone, report to your squad leaders in thirty. Dismissed."

The chopper was approaching its island target. It was easy for Joe and the rest of the team to know where they were going. The black oil fumes were still covering the landing zone. They actually appeared to be thicker than they had been when the surveillance photo was taken. The Black Hawk pilot came over the helmet radio.

"I thought the commander said that cloud was going to be gone by the time we arrived."

"I guess not," Joe answered. "Do you think the rotor wash will blow some of it away?"

"Not sure, I'll try it though. After infil, I'll buzz it and see if it has an effect."

"Roger.

Just five more minutes and the chopper was hovering over the smoke. Under the helicopter, a clear patch of ground appeared, blown clear by the choppers wind wash.

"Go! Go! Go!" Joe commanded his troops out of the Black Hawk. Black ropes unfurled out the side, and men rappelled down. Joe took one look to the west, where another team was rappelling to the other side of the road, and slid down the rope himself. As soon as the last man was on the ground, the chopper pilot pulled higher into the sky.

"Captain Feller?"

Joe put his hand to his ear to better hear the call from the pilot. The buzz of the engines almost drowned out the call.

"Captain Feller?"

"This is Captain Feller. On ground, over."

"Captain Feller, negative on wind blast runs. The smoke is too thick. Experiencing engine clogging, over."

"Fire-support capability?

"Negative. Zero visibility, and the zombies aren't reading on thermals."

Joe cursed under his breath. "Roger." Something was wrong about this whole thing. Joe's sixth sense was screaming at him. They were just zombies though. This wasn't a war zone. He shook the doubts from his consciousness.

The pilot came back over the radio. "Find that fire causing the smoke and extinguish it, and you'll get your air support. I'll stay close by."

"Roger. Out."

This mission just became a lot worse. The light still made it through the smoke, but just barely. It felt like twilight. Joe was reminded of when his brother, Kurt, and he would play the local golf course as teenagers. They would hop on just as the sun was setting and try to finish as many holes as possible before it got too dark. Usually the last hole they played was a game of luck with finding their balls. That was the feeling now. He could make out shapes and general images but not specific details. Whatever was causing this smoke needed to be found and doused, fast.

"Let's hurry, men. Spread out and move forward. I don't want to be stuck on a zombie-infested island without any support in this haze," Joe shouted out his commands. He then thought to himself: *The mission was supposed to be as simple as securing a bridge after dropping practically on top of the damn thing.*

Joe called the other fire team commander. "This smoke is going to make bridging an issue, plus I don't like having no air support. You and your team, hold position and clear those trees. We'll move forward and extinguish whatever is burning and regroup at the bridge. Roger?"

"Aye aye," the response chirped through the radio.

Joe laughed, thinking, *okay, Navy.* "On me!" Joe commanded. "Let's find the source of this smoke and stop it."

"How are we supposed to put it out?" asked Martinell. Joe had grown to like him over the last months of fighting. He was a good kid.

"Hopefully it's a small fuel leak and we can just bury it, suffocate the fire in the process. Worst-case scenario, we set charges near the source and detonate. It would be dangerous, depending on the source, but it would exhaust all the fuel quickly."

Martinell and the other eight men all nodded their heads.

"Martinell, you're on point. Move out, let's this get done and get out of this place."

Martinell took the first position as the fire team moved out in a small column. They marched toward the thickest part of the smoke cloud.

Every step quickly became a struggle. The air was dousing the group with unburned oil in the form of a black steam. It caked their uniforms. Each soldier had to tie rags over his face to just breathe without chocking on the black oil. Tears of black ran down some of the men's faces as their eyes rejected the liquid. The air burned the men's eyes and nostrils. The toxic smog became hotter with every step the column took toward the source. After 250 meters, Martinell called, "Hold!" from the front. Joe ran up to where he was crouched, looking at the dirt.

Joe took a knee by Martinell and looked up at the young man. Martinell began motioning with his hands. He pointed two fingers at his eyes and then pointed those same fingers at the ground. Joe followed the path to where his fingers ended up pointing. He saw what had caused Martinell distress.

The ground had a clear cut through the mud heading to the source of the smoke. The ground had been plowed deep. These could be only one thing: drag marks. Drag marks seemed strange. Maybe something had been sent sliding along the ground during the bombing. Maybe someone had dragged something before this whole zombie thing happened. Maybe Joe was grasping at straws. Whatever caused these marks, the mission didn't change.

Joe looked up at Martinell. Martinell was scanning through the fog, trying to pierce the cloud with his eyes, attempting to see anything other than the oily fog. Joe hit him on the shoulder, getting his attention. Joe gave him the hand signal for "follow me." Joe took point as the column moved forward cautiously. Joe was following the drag marks.

About fifty meters further into the smoke, Joe and the column of men found the source of the fire. Set in a semicircle was a ring of oil tankers. Each was leaking fuel from its tapping spout into a pit in a steady stream. At the bottom of the ten-foot-deep pit was a raging fire. About thirty tanks fueled the fire. This was not an accident of any kind. This fire was built. Something was wrong. Joe broke the radio silence.

"Bravo team, come in."

The radio chirped as the leader of Bravo came over the radio. "Bravo. Report. Did you find the source?"

"Yes, but something's wrong. We are marking the coordinates for a bombing run. We are exfilling now! Keep your eyes peeled. I think we may have walked into a trap."

"Zombies that set traps? Are you kidding?"

"Negative. It looks that way."

Bravo's response was a four-letter foul word.

"Roger. We are coming to you, and we are getting off this island. Alpha out."

Joe then called the helicopter, relayed all the information and arranged for the exfil boat.

Joe had taken two steps before he heard the chatter of automatic rifles coming through the smoke. The click-and-clack was muffled but definite. Joe gave the "HOLD" sign and got back on the radio. "Bravo, report! Bravo, report!"

"THEY'RE COMING OUT OF THE TREES! OUT OF THE F-ING TREES!"

The gunfire increased in intensity.

"Bravo, say again."

Silence.

"Bravo, say again!"

There was no answer.

The sound of gunfire was still ringing out. Joe strained to see through the smoke. Somewhere out there, Bravo team was fighting for their lives.

Bravo's leader, a tall, slender captain named Perld, yelled to his men, giving the order to move out of the trees and head for the road.

Immediately after Perld yelled the order to move out, the trees started moving. Bravo team had held their positions as the trees started to shake, dropping coconuts to the ground. A high-pitched whining combined with the sound of grinding choked out everything else. The air was thick with the sound, even thicker than the smoke. Then as the auditory assault reached a painful crescendo, it stopped. Everything stopped shaking, except the legs of the men in Bravo squad. One of the men, farthest from Captain Perld, deep in the trees, yelled out to his commander, "Sir, what is this?"

In response, the trees around him burst. A zombie came flying out of every tree close to the man. The undead descended on the man. He only fired one shot before three zombies had sunk their teeth into him.

The two men closest to the poor man currently being enjoyed as a buffet were the first to raise their rifles. They opened up with automatic fire. Their guns blasted. The zombies were ripped to shreds from the discharge. As the guns fired, the trees next to the men exploded with zombie assailants pouring out of them as well. The two men were soon the center of zombie feeding circles.

As the men attempted to survive, the other two men of the fire squad opened fire. The pattern continued. The gunfire ringing out from their rifles set off the trap. The undead came flying out of the hollowed-out palm trees like they were shot out of cannons. Soon the spatter of gunfire and screaming zombies were all that could be heard. Three of the men, somehow still alive, had gotten back to back and were doing all they could to survive.

Captain Perld had recognized what was happening and knew, despite his greatest desires, he couldn't help his men. If he fired his weapon, the trees close to him would explode with the undead. Perld had lain down in a prone position to avoid getting hit by a stray round as the men fought. This was worse torture for him than anything, watching his men fight for their lives, unable to help. He had to report what was happening, or it would happen to the next group.

As Captain Perld grinded his teeth in agony, his problem was solved. The radio attached to his pack chirped static and then a loud, demanding voice. As soon as Captain Feller's voice came over the radio, "Bravo, report! Bravo, report!" the trees next to Captain Perld erupted with zombie assailants. Perld's prone position gave him the second to get his message out before the zombies found the source of the noise.

"THEY'RE COMING OUT OF THE TREES! OUT OF THE F-ING TREES!" He screamed over the radio and opened up with his M16.

"Bravo, report! Bravo, report!"

The only answer was the gunfire raging through the smoke. Someone was still fighting. A few seconds later, everything stopped. Silence reigned.

Joe put the handheld radio away. Alpha needed to get moving. Joe waved for everyone to follow him. They took off at a light jogging pace, covering twice the ground of a normal walk with each stride. They were moving quickly to get to the exfil point. They were moving too quickly. Joe heard the cracking a split second before the ground gave way.

In their haste, they had walked onto a pitfall. The ground had been dug out from underneath, leaving only a small patch of dirt supported by pieces of wood. On the way to the source, they had maintained separation. Because of this, their combined weight hadn't been on the trap at once. On their fast-paced journey back, the group's spacing had become too close.

As the trap sprung, all the members of Alpha fell, grabbing at the air, into a twelve-foot-deep hole. Joe shook his head, clearing the ringing out of his ears, and looked around. The walls had been hand dug at an inward-sloping angle, making climbing out impossible. The round enclosure had a set of tunnels leading out of it. Joe had an idea what these tunnels were for. "360 security!" He yelled in a terrified tone. Joe and his men formed a circle with their backs to each other, looking outward, waiting.

The tunnels started humming. The rhythmic tones of screaming came echoing out. The noise grew in strength, stinging their eardrums. They were under an audio assault. Next, foul smells hit Alpha squad. It was a breeze of death and decay coming out of each tunnel, an air cannon of putridity. Then the real attack began. White teeth and exposed bone glowed in the dark of the tunnels and the underground pit. Alpha opened fire. Their only chance was to clog up the tunnels. Screams and gunfire reverberated off the walls of the room. Bullets tore through greenish, rotting skin. Heads exploded, and limbs detached. Magazines and bullet casings hit the floor as Alpha unleashed all they had. After two minutes of pure mayhem, everything stopped.

It was a pause in the battle.

"Check ammo!" Joe called out loud in the silence. Everyone's ears were ringing, and they could barely hear him.

Because of this, they did not hear the grinding of bone against rock. The walls around them erupted in dirt and undead tunnelers. A new set of tunnels had been made. Again Alpha opened with everything they had. The blasts were deafening in such a small area.

These tunnels were twice as large as before, allowing two zombies to walk next to each other.

Alpha poured all they could into the fight. One man threw a perfect grenade, collapsing a tunnel but killing himself in the process. The blast had followed the tunnel and sent a shock wave in a concentrated column right back at him.

As the men fought a losing battle, their ammunition began to run low. The circle of men became smaller and smaller. Soon it was only Joe and Martinell left. They were back to back, spinning in a circle of death, keeping the undead at bay. The zombies pulled back to regroup for their finishing offensive.

Their time was running out. Martinell ran out of ammo first. Joe handed him the last mag of handgun ammo he had.

"This is it," Joe said.

Martinell looked at Joe with a determined look in his eyes. "Sir, we need to get out of here.

Joe just looked at him, his face saying, it's not happening.

Martinell had other ideas. "Sir, you have long arms."

Joe was confused. "So?"

"If I give you a boost out of here and you reach back down, I should be able to jump and catch your grip."

Joe looked up at the ground ceiling. It seemed plausible. The roof had lowered a whole foot where the tunnel collapse had occurred. "Can you hold me?"

"Yes, sir."

Joe quickly dropped all his gear, so he was just in his bare uniform. He needed to lighten the load. He stepped onto Martinell's knee and up onto his shoulders. Joe waved his arms as Martinell stood up. Joe reached up and grabbed onto a piece of wood that supported the ground near the edge of the pit. It was solid. He pulled himself out of the hole. Joe turned around, reached his hand out. Martinell took a few steps back and then began running.

One step, two steps, Martinell planted and pushed with all his might. As he went airborne, a hand grabbed him. It wasn't Joe's.

A zombie had come rushing out of the tunnel and dove at Martinell. He caught him midair. Martinell's fingers had touched the tips of Joe's, but he was too short on his leap. Martinell came crashing to the ground as Joe had to watch. The zombie tore into Martinell's lower legs, its teeth digging through clothes and skin, and into bone. Martinell screamed and started fumbling with his pack. He looked up at Joe and screamed, "RUN!"

Joe saw why. Martinell had pulled out the C4 plastic explosive they had planned to use to blow the fuel. He would go out fighting. Joe crawled backward away from the edge. He turned and took a few steps, running toward the beach. The ground became a wave under his feet. It lurched and dipped. All around him, dirt erupted into the air. The explosion followed the tunnels. Any weak point became a geyser of dirt, air and dead flesh.

The concussion and moving ground threw Joe to the earth. He was already disoriented from the underground battle. This explosion threw him into complete confusion. Joe could only focus on one thought: *Get to the beach. Get to the ocean.*

He crawled. He could feel the sand as his fingers pushed through soil. Crawling, just crawling. Joe was a zombie himself now. Blood ran from his ears, nose and eyes. He was fighting against becoming unconscious. He felt the cool lap of water on his fingers. With a couple more exertive drags, he was floating in the water. Joe began backstroking as best he could. He looked up at the sky, seeing the smoke floating away from that cursed island. The smoke billowed and played in his vision. Soon it was all he could see.

Everything went black.

Chapter 3

The Russian Wilderness:
Outbreak Day +65

Twigs snapped underfoot as Kurt ran as fast as the terrain allowed through the dense Russian forest. The trees flew by like a blur as he ducked under branches and hopped over the occasional downed tree. Kurt was careful. He had trail run before and knew one wrong step could result in a broken ankle. If he slowed now, he would be dead.

The zombie pursuing him was not nearly as agile, but it also hadn't given up. Black, bloody ooze ran from its shattered ankles and a million cuts along its upper body. This man had been dead and buried for years, but the permafrost of the Russian soil had kept his body preserved. This natural mummy was now brought back to life and was hungry. Kurt had built himself a near-three-hundred-yard advantage. Hearing a loud snap, he turned around. The zombie was gone.

Kurt got down on one knee. His heart was pounding through his ears. The *thump-thump-thump* deafened him and blocked out any noises from the surrounding forest. He had to focus on his breathing

to calm his body. Eyes still darting all around, he
rested for a few minutes.

His breath and heart now back to resting rate,
Kurt could finally hear it. The zombie was still out
there. Its moans and screams were now different,
muted, muffled. It sounded like someone gagging.
Kurt slowly got up and walked cautiously toward the
noise. After a short time, he reached his undead
pursuer.

The zombie was lying down on the ground,
face first. It was scratching at the dirt, trying to crawl
but couldn't. Its right leg was broken at the knee.
Kneecap and femur stuck out of the pale skin. The
other leg of the zombie was shattered above the ankle,
where the teeth of a bear trap now clamped down. It
was trapped, literally. When it had fallen, its jaw had
slammed into a rock, also shattering. The permafrost
had preserved the zombie's body, but this used-to-be-
man's bones were brittle. It now only had one jaw and
was trying to scream but only could manage a gurgle.
It saw Kurt and started crawling in his direction. Kurt
took a step back. The zombie now was at the end of
its leash, a few feet from its prey. Yet it still grabbed
and clawed at the dirt underfoot.

Kurt looked at the pathetic form lying there
and felt a strange feeling. It was a mix of hatred,
adrenaline and pity. This thing was a killer who would
have eaten Kurt like a gourmet meal at the first
chance, but it still wasn't the zombie's fault. It hadn't
chosen to take Enerjax. It was a buried soul in a mass,
unmarked grave. This man probably died in one of the

great wars. He deserved peace. Instead he got to come back and become an undead murderer in his next life. Either his karma was shit or he was a victim once again. Whatever soul occupied this body before didn't earn a life as a zombie. He also was going to attract others with that noise.

Kurt held Philip's gun and pointed it at the trapped zombie's head. *Too loud,* he thought. He tucked the gun into his waistband. Kurt looked around until he found a good rock. He took a step toward the zombie rolling on the ground in front of him, planning on smashing the stone into its head. As soon as he got close, the zombie reared up and flung both bony hands in Kurt's direction. Kurt barely jumped back in time. This creature still had some fight in him. Kurt couldn't get too close. He steadied himself and threw the stone with all his might. He missed, hitting the zombie in the back. He cringed, "Oops, sorry man." He grabbed another couple of stones and took better aim. This time, the throw hit dead center of the zombie's skull, fracturing it. The zombie's arms flailed at a much slower rate than before. Clearly the impact had hurt its capacity. Kurt took this opportunity, bringing down another rock, this time from much closer. The impact sent the stone all the way through its head and into the leafy mud. Black blood mixed with rotting leaves. Kurt covered his nose and stepped back, retreating from the putrid scent.

Kurt turned away from the scene beneath him and headed back into the forest, this time at a much slower pace, hoping to avoid the same fate. *Watch for bear traps, check.* It was just another danger to look out for in this new zombie world. A few hundred feet farther into the forest, Kurt stepped over the early alarm system of bells, officially leaving the settlement behind.

Florida Keys: Outbreak Day +64

Bright lights burned Joe's vision, and his eyes weren't even open. He could see the orange, reddish glow through his closed eyelids. Joe felt the warmth scorching on his skin.

Oh my god, Joe thought. *I'm dead. I must be. When I open my eyes, what will I see? I can feel the heat. Is that a good or bad thing? Am I in the good place, or have the souls of those I killed condemned me?*

Joe readied his mind and, with all his effort, attempted to open his eyes. No matter what he tried, he couldn't. They were stuck shut. Joe wanted to panic, but the rest of him seemed completely unresponsive. He was trapped in his head.

What do I do? Think, you idiot. You must not be dead. There is no way that God or the devil would let you see or feel nothing. Well maybe the second would? No, that wouldn't be torture enough. Maybe this is just death? What if when you die, you simply stay stuck in limbo forever? A feeling of fear came over Joe's mind. *Well if that's true, then there's nothing I can do. Are there any other options? Well I guess I could have been rescued from that ocean. If I were, I would be in rough shape. I could be on an operating table right now. Sometimes they tape the eyes shut to keep them moist. That's a possibility at least. Okay, as long as there is a possibility I may be alive, then I'm not giving up. I'm going to keep fighting. There are people out there who need you. Think of them, Joe.* Kira's face came to the forefront of Joe's mind. He watched her as she spoke to him. He relived his conversation with her. *"You promised, Joe. You promised you'd come back to me. Say it. Say it again."* I promise. Next, Kurt appeared. *"Don't leave me alone out here, bro. I need you. You have to save me."* I'll find you. I will. I promise. I promise. I promise. Joe recited his promise in his mind continuously. As he did, his sense of fear changed to one of determination. Soon Joe felt an immense feeling of exhaustion overtaking him. He fought to stay awake a little longer, to foster this feeling of unwavering drive, but eventually sleep came.

Joe fought against the sleep. He opened his eyes and squinted against the brightness. The sun was shining brightly in the midday sky. Birds chirped, and bugs flitted away as Joe and Kurt jogged down a Florida hiking trail. The humidity stuck to their bodies as both ran shirtless along the path. The parking lot was only a quarter-mile away. Joe smiled at Kurt, and Kurt nodded back. They both took off in a dead sprint, racing each other. They were dead even. Both looked at each other, smiling, a challenge between two loving brothers. Joe felt like he hadn't

seen his brother in some time. He was so happy. They tied as they came thundering into the gravel parking zone. Joe slowed up. Kurt continued on and touched the car.

"First!" Kurt squeezed out the word under labored breaths. He put his hands on his knees and bent over. The final push had emptied his tanks.

Joe was walking toward the car with his hands on his hips. He caught his breath faster than Kurt. "The race was to the parking lot."

Kurt stood tall now. "No, the race is always to the car."

"Since when?" Joe laughed.

"Since today." They both smiled.

Joe walked closer to his brother. "I miss you, man."

"I miss you too, bro."

Joe leaned against the car, lying back on top of the hood, soaking in the sun. The car began beeping. Joe stood up quickly and pulled out the car key. He went to press the alarm button. Before he did, a voice interrupted him.

"What are you doing?" Kurt was looking at him questioningly.

Joe responded like he had just been asked the dumbest question ever. "Turning off the car alarm."

"What car alarm?" Kurt remained confused.

"The one in front of us." Joe answered condescendingly.

Kurt turned around in a circle, searching for any alarm.

Joe was now the one confused. "Wait, you don't hear that?"

Kurt asked, "Hear what?" He put his arms out to his side, indicating he did not.

"That constant beeping. You're joking, right? It sounds like . . ." Joe trailed off.

Kurt asked back. "Sounds like what?"
Joe stammered, "Like, like . . ."
The world around him dissolved to black.

Florida Keys: Outbreak Day +65

Joe opened his eyes in a hospital room. He rolled his head to the side and looked at the heart rate monitor. It beeped at a constant pace. Seeing it, Joe began to understand. As he woke from his deep sleep, the monitor began beeping faster and faster. A nurse ran in, straight to the machine. She turned and looked at Joe's open eyes, and recognition flared. The nurse turned off the machine's sound and looked at Joe.

"Welcome back. How do you feel?" The nurse's name tag read "Ricard." She was a larger woman in her early fifties or late forties. She was wearing a pair of simple, teal-blue scrubs.

Joe answered with the only thing he could at that moment. "Like I want to be back asleep." He had felt joy and love in his sleep. There was no place for that in this world. The world was an evil place.

"I don't blame you, especially after all that happened. Rest up. I'll let the commander know you pulled through."

Joe stared at the drop ceiling as tears poured down his cheeks. Images of men dying and Martinell's outstretched hand began playing like a twisted slideshow. The final image was that of his brother looking into the void as Joe had been pulled from the dream. Joe cried himself back to sleep.

The next morning when he woke up, after a dreamless night, the nurse was in the room, adjusting the flow of the IV into his arm.

"What are you doing?" Joe asked.

She answered back in a good-mannered tone. "Good morning. I am turning down your anesthetic so that you can start moving around on your own. You're still going to be here in bed for a few days. The damage you sustained wasn't too extensive."

Joe looked down at the hospital blanket that covered everything but his arms. His arms had some cuts and bandages on them. What did that cloth hide? What was underneath?

Reading the fear in Joe's eyes, Nurse Ricard chimed in. "The worst of it was a concussion. You did have some shrapnel pieces that punctured your back as well as a bullet that pierced your leg. You were in surgery for a few hours. Luckily for you, a talented surgeon had just retired and was visiting his family in the Keys when the outbreak occurred. He said he knew you. He said you saved him. He said that you had pulled his family and him off a roof a few months ago."

Joe thought of the elderly man he had saved on one of his first missions. Maybe karma was real.

The nurse continued. "He was able to close up your bullet wound and get all the shrapnel out with only one incision. You will only have a small scar to remember it all by, the size of a quarter on your back.

Luckily the shrapnel was all localized, so he was able to do an arthroscopic surgery. I'm sure you're curious about what that is. Basically we puffed your body up a little with gas, and he was able to reach all the metal pieces through that single small incision. You'll recover quickly. Just a few days here in the hospital and you'll be on your way. You will have some pain there for a while, but not terrible, which is good because we can't spare painkillers. The only downside is that you may fart a little as the gas works its way out, but you'll survive. As for those around you, they may not." Nurse Ricard giggled a little.

Joe twitched his right index finger. The nurse noticed his struggle. "Good, you're already regaining movement in your extremities. It won't be long until you can sit up."

"What is that stuff, Nurse Ricard? I've been put under before, but something's different about that serum. My head is still clear. Usually when you get put under by drugs, you feel messed up."

She smiled back, "When were you put under?"

Joe responded, "A couple times." He didn't know how to answer that question. Joe could have told her about the wisdom-tooth surgery that had complications, or the time he broke his ankle as a kid while trail running with his brother, or the training to resist enemy interrogation using pharmaceuticals in Special Forces.

"Well it's an older drug. As you can imagine, we don't have an endless supply of the good stuff."

"Why don't they use it anymore?"

Nurse Ricard's smile vanished. "Well it can have some side effects if you're not careful.

"Side effects?"

"Oh, don't worry, it's not like you won't be able to love a woman again or anything. For one, because you're clearheaded. Sometimes people seem to give up on life and accept death. Sometimes when they wake up, they reject the world around them as real."

"Wow." Joe thought back to his inner discussion with himself.

"That's not the worst. If the dose is too high, even a little bit, the drug can burn out nerves, leaving areas of your body senseless. Or if left too high for too long, it can result in paralysis. In some cases, of the heart and lungs."

"So this stuff can kill me?"

"Yes. That's why we've been monitoring you so closely and are now taking you off it."

"Sounds good to me. Take it out of my arm, Nurse."

"I wish it were that simple."

"Is it not?"

"We have to slowly dial it down or you may go into withdrawals."

"I like the plan of weaning me off it," Joe said.

"Me too. Now rest. When you wake up, you'll feel a lot like your old self again."

"Thanks."

Nurse Ricard smiled politely back.

Joe closed his eyes. He prayed to dream of Kurt again.

Florida Keys: Outbreak Day +66

It was late night when Joe woke from his sleep. He hadn't dreamt at all again. What a waste. The orange-tinted hospital lights cast a burnt pallor over everything. Joe looked around the room. It took him a few seconds to notice the man sitting in the chair in the corner. The man was sitting with a notebook, rubbing something metal in his hands.

Joe pushed himself to a seated position. His arms had regained most of their strength. His legs were still numb. As he pushed himself up on the pillow, he let out a muffled groan. That "small pain" in his back was a little worse than Nurse Ricard had let on. The man in the corner looked up from whatever he was working on.

"You're awake.

Joe coughed out some remainders of his sleep and, with a dry throat, responded, "Yeah."

The man stood up and grabbed a cup of water on the bed stand. He handed it to Joe. "Here."

"Thank you." The water had been sitting out for some time and become lukewarm. It didn't matter. The water soothed Joe's cracked and parched throat. "I think I need a new IV."

"Oh, the nurse said they aren't going to give you any more. Something about saving them for emergencies. I guess that means you're recovering well."

"Yeah, I guess so." Joe looked absentmindedly at the wall in front of him. He shook his head, dislodging the last few cobwebs from his nap. "I'm sorry, who are you?"

The man shifted his notebook to his other hand. "Hi, my name is Kevin, I'm here to take your after-action report."

"My report, are you serious? Can't they wait until I can type it myself?"

"I'm afraid not. The faster we take care of this the faster you get to sleep."

Something about this guy rubbed Joe the wrong way. His "Spidey sense" was tingling.

"What branch are you in?"

"Oh, I'm not military."

Joe grew more suspicious.

"I'm a civilian volunteer. My brother is in . . . well I guess, *was* in the military." A clear hurt came over his face. He glanced down at the object he was playing with earlier. Joe saw it clearly for the first time. It was a dog tag. "Well he . . . he died. The Army asked me to help, but I couldn't fight. I have epilepsy, and explosions or gunfire triggers it. So I volunteered to help in any other way I can."

Joe read the man in front of him. There were no lies in his words. "So you're not a reporter or some blogger trying to get the details of our first failed mission?"

"No. I'm just here to take your statement."

"Okay, but can you answer me a question first."

"Sure."

"How did I get here?"

"Your, I guess you call it an 'exfiltration boat,' well it came to pick you all up. It saw the massive explosion and high-tailed it to shore. When they arrived, no one was there. One of the men spotted you in the waves, floating to sea. They pulled you out. You were still breathing. Then you were rushed here."

Joe nodded. "Okay, where . . . where do I need to start?"

"Start from when you left the helicopter."

As Joe relived one of the worst days of his life in explicit detail, Kevin sat quietly and took notes, only asking the occasional question, clarifying events. After Joe had painfully explained everything, Kevin closed his notebook and stood pacing near the foot of Joe's bed.

"Why?" Kevin asked as he stopped.

Joe asked back, "Why what?"

"Why did you leave Specialist Eddie Martinell in that hole?"

Joe became defensive. "Leave him? Are you joking? Did you listen to anything I said?"

"Why didn't you lift him out first and then jump up to him yourself?"

"He didn't have long enough arms to reach down."

"Why didn't Eddie climb up over you once you had caught the wood?"

"I guess the board couldn't have held us both. We made a split-second call. What we tried was the only chance for both of us to live."

Kevin sat back down in the chair, hunched over, rubbing the dog tag. "You guess? He started to rub the dog tag he was holding, his breathing audibly growing fast. He grabbed the dog tag hard. His breathing slowed, and he sat back down, oddly calm all of a sudden. Do you have a brother, Captain Feller?"

"Yes."

"Is he here with you in the Keys?"

"No."

"Where is he?"

"Russia."

"Is he alive?"

"Yes."

"How do you know? You've been out for a couple of days. Are you in communication with him? I saw your sat phone is still working." Kevin pointed at a table in the corner of the room. Joe's possessions sat on the table, including the satellite phone. "I'm amazed it survived the salt water. Yet it works just fine. I took the liberty of charging it while you were sleeping. How lucky you are. Have you two been talking?"

"No. But I know he's alive. I just do. I just know."

Kevin still stared at the dog tag. "I know what you mean." He looked up with tears in his eyes. "Let me tell you a story."

Kevin sat back in the chair but never broke eye contact with the steel in his hands. "Once upon a time, a recent time, there were two brothers. They

loved each other very much. One brother became a
software engineer in New York, while the other joined
the military. Even though they may have chosen
different lives, they would talk every day. They made
plans for the future. One day, one glorious day, they
would live close to each other. Their kids would play
together in backyards and on the same T-ball teams.
The two brothers were separated for the moment, but
it wasn't going to last. Do you know why? Because
they were covenant brothers. They were always there
for each other when one needed the other." Kevin
had been smiling while telling this part of the story.
His face glazed over with happy emotions. In an
instant, those emotions and the blood drained from
his face. "Then something happened. The world
changed. Zombies became a thing and began attacking
everything. Mayhem plunged the globe into a survival
mode. Well the two brothers had no way of contacting
each other. Even if they did, they didn't have the time.
Each of the two brothers was fighting and running
and doing things they would regret for the rest of their
lives. None of that mattered though. Anything that
ensured survival was necessary, not just for a selfish
desire to live but, more importantly, to live for the
other brother. Well after a long time and a lot of
struggle, the brother in New York made his way down
the coast and ended up here, in the Florida Keys.
Compared to what he saw up north, he realized these
people had no idea what was going on. He envied
them. Their innocence, their ignorance, and most of
all, he envied the families. Brothers played together on

sandy beaches, throwing a football back and forth,
and talking about the future. What had they done to
deserve something that great? Did that brother not
sacrifice? Did he not love enough? Why? Why was he
destined for such a torture?"

Joe swallowed a large amount of saliva that had
built up in his throat. The man sitting in the chair was
starting to become more and more agitated. "Hey, you
know, you don't have to tell me this story."

"Don't interrupt!" Kevin's countenance was
breaking. He continued. "Well after nearly a week, this
brother decided that he couldn't sit around or fish,
just living like nothing had happened. So he did the
one thing he could. He decided to help the efforts to
kill the zombies that had separated his brother and
him. You see, he never thought his brother was dead.
He couldn't explain why, but he had hope. There was
something in his soul that told him his brother was
alive, out there fighting somewhere. This brother had
to find him. His prayers were answered. Once he
signed up as a volunteer, he discovered his brother
was not only alive, but he was there with him. They
were literally in the same city, at the same military
base. They were about to be reunited after such a long
and painful journey. Their story was about to have a
happy ending. Then just before I could find him, he
was sent on a mission to the north. But I was told not
to worry, he would be back later that day. His mission
was led by an amazing captain. So it was only a few
more hours of separation." Kevin took a deep breath.
As he did, his shoulders hunched over and his chin

began wavering. "My brother, Eddie Martinell, didn't make it home. In fact, only one man did."

Joe's eyes grew five sizes larger. His sixth sense erupted. He reached for the nurse alarm button. Before he could grab it, Kevin was out of his chair. He grabbed Joe's hand and cupped it between his.

"No. No. The story isn't over yet. Do you know who that man was?"

Joe was still weak from the anesthetic and surgery. He tried to free his hand from Kevin's grasp, but he couldn't.

"That's right. Just that amazing captain."

Joe tried something else, pleading. "I'm sorry. I'm so sorry. Martinell was a good man. We . . . we didn't know what was happening on that island. It wasn't my fault."

"Not your fault? Oh, I know. I don't hold you responsible for his death. I heard your story. There really was nothing you could have done other than scrub the mission from the start. Then again, you had never witnessed zombie strategy before. You didn't realize they hunted in packs and even used tools. It's not your fault."

Joe saw something sinister lurking in the back of Kevin's eyes. "Listen, I don't think—"

Kevin tightened his grip and stared at his hands. "You have to let me finish my story." Kevin leaned against the bed. "Where was I? Oh, that's right, one brother was dead. The other brother, me, was left with the knowledge that he would never see his brother again. He had lost a loved one. He had lost a chance at that dream future. But you know what else he lost in that moment?" Kevin looked up at Joe, making direct eye contact. His face was not one of anger but one of sad depression. "He lost his hope. You see, without that chance of finding his brother, the world was only an evil place. Sure, evil things had happened, but with the hope of finding Eddie alive, I always had a reason for the pain. Something to push toward. Now I have nothing. I am an empty shell. That pain is the hardest thing I've ever experienced. I would have killed myself by now, but I heard that you were alive, and I had to come meet the man who got Eddie killed. I thought I would hate you, but I don't. I envy you. You have what I lost. You have hope. You have given me a new purpose. I must make people realize. I must help others understand how dangerous hope is. Only with no hope can we actually move on. Only without hope can we survive without getting hurt. Hope is our enemy in this new world. I must destroy that curse. I must set others free, and you will be my first success. It's beautiful, isn't it? You chose to join the military. You chose to sacrifice to allow others to live freely. Now you will do the same. You will be the first to feel what it's like to lose hope and be set free from it. I will be the one to save you. And I will tell the story of how you escaped the cruelty of this world and how now you are at peace to the rest of those I help. How you finally were no longer a prisoner of hope."

Kevin reached up and turned the flow of the anesthetic to its max levels. The effect was instant. Joe felt his arm becoming numb, radiating from the point of the IV injection. After just a few seconds, Kevin didn't need to hold his hand anymore. As Joe returned to the prison in his body, Kevin stood up and placed his brother's dog tag onto the bedside table. He gathered his notebook and walked to the door. Kevin turned as he left, turning off the light. Pausing in the doorway, he faced Joe directly.

"Thank you for your service."

Kevin left, closing the door behind him. Joe screamed inside his mind. He was trapped. Soon the only real sensation he had was his hearing. Even that was filled with a ringing, a musical tone.

That ringing, it sounded familiar. It had stopped after a short while, followed by a beep. Joe was trying to stay awake, using the mystery to keep him from sleeping, and alive. What felt like an eternity passed. The door to his room burst open and slammed shut.

"Why aren't you dead yet!"

Joe couldn't open his eyes, but he recognized the voice. It was Kevin. He was back. Joe screamed in his mind. He could hear Kevin's breathing. Joe could hear a knife being unsheathed. Then Joe heard a blast, a gunshot exploding through the window. Glass tinkled across the floor. Then silence.

"Joe, are you okay?" It was Nurse Ricard. Joe recognized the accent.

Joe screamed *yes* in his mind.

"If you're okay, move your eyes back and forth."

Joe looked left and then right. They must have moved enough to show through the eyelids. Nurse Ricard sighed and said, "You're going to be all right."

A day and a half later, Joe was up and walking. The only side effect of his overdose on the anesthetic was numbing around his surgical scar. In a weird way, Kevin had saved him from pain. Joe gave nurse Ricard a farewell hug as he walked out the front doors of the hospital. A jeep was waiting to take him home. He had never looked so forward to seeing Kira and the kids. She and those children were examples of the purity still remaining in this twisted world. He loved them. He would never let them go.

He also had a new piece of information. His faith had been rewarded. Now he really had hope.

Key West Harbor: Outbreak Day +68

Kira returned from yet another successful day of fishing. She exchanged her catch for gas and fishing tackle. After another comical haggle with Frannie, she headed back home to the *La Vida Dulce*.

Kira pulled past the row of boats. She waved at an older man shaking out a rug on the bow of his ship. He glared and turned away, shaking his rug in a different direction. *What is going on?* Kira thought. *When we first got here, everyone was so nice. Now they won't even wave hello.* Proving her exact thoughts, Kira spotted a pair of eyes watching her through the blinds of a houseboat's window. When Kira made eye contact, the blinds abruptly shut. *The weather is starting to warm, but the people sure as heck aren't.*

Kira pulled her boat up to *La Vida Dulce* and tied it up. She climbed onto the back deck of the yacht and surveyed the chain of boats docked together. It was a ghost town. She felt eerie watching the docks sway in the waves of a lightly rocking sea. Something felt twisted. Kira turned and went inside. The second she stepped inside, all negative feelings melted away and the kids ran to her and threw their arms around her legs, hugging away all the strangeness.

"Miss Kira!" they all cheered in unison.

"Kira, can we play outside today?" Elizabeth asked.

"Yeah, please!" Jack added.

"Not today, kids, it's a little wavy out there," Kira answered.

"Ahh!" they all echoed. "It's because the other people hate us, isn't it?" Christine asked.

"The other people don't hate us!" Jack said.

"Yeah-huh! We did something wrong, and now they don't like us." Christine snapped back.

"Is that true, Miss Kira?" Jack asked with sadness on his face.

Kira knelt down and looked at the three small faces. "No. No, kids, you didn't do anything wrong, and people don't hate you."

"Then why do they look at us so angry?" Christine asked. "Last time we played outside, Mrs. Ophelia even slammed her door shut."

"Yeah!" Elizabeth echoed.

"Listen, kids, I don't know why everyone has stopped coming out and being nice, but it has nothing to do with you."

"That's not what Mrs. Perld next door said," Christine retorted.

"What do you mean?" Kira asked, surprised.

"Well the other day, I could hear her through the window. She was on the phone, crying. Then she was yelling. Then she said that we were lucky little brats who don't deserve everything. She said that everything we did reminded her of how much she lost. She said we made her sad." Christine frowned and hung her head. "She said worse things about you."

Kira was taken aback. "Well, kids, I don't know what's going on with her, but I'm going over there to straighten this out. First we need to have breakfast." Kira forced a smile onto her face. "I brought home eggs today. You know what that means." She raised her eyebrows excitedly.

"Momlets!" Jack exclaimed. The other children instantly grew big smiles.

Kira laughed, "Yes, it's omelet time."

Kira had finished cleaning all the dishes after a messy breakfast with the kids. They had all gone downstairs to play. It was time to figure out what was going on with Mrs. Perld next door. She walked the short distance and knocked on her back door.

Mrs. Perld answered the door. She was a mess. Her eyes were bloodshot, and the trails of tears down her face were easily visible. "What do you want from me? Don't you have enough?"

Kira let the insulting tone slide. "I wanted to check on you. The kids said they heard you crying."

"Sure! Yeah, I was crying. So now you've come to rub salt in the wound?"

Kira lost her patience. "What are you talking about?!"

"You know!" Mrs. Perld spat back at her.

Kira was genuinely hurt. "Look, I don't know. I don't get it. You and I both have been ostracized for the last few months from everyone else. You and I have both felt the judging and peering eyes of everyone, just because we have two men close to us alive and fighting up north. Like we didn't lose others. You and I both chose to relocate to this far end of the boat dock to get away from it, that bullshit jealousy. Now you're turning on me now too. Why?"

"Why?" Mrs. Perld was turning hateful. "Why? Because you're a reminder. You and your little 'family' are a reminder of everything that I have lost. I have held on long enough. I have watched your 'kids' playing outside. I have listened to their laughing and seen the smile on your face. I have watched you tie those barrels to the front of your boat, and I have seen you bring home gift after gift after gift from your fishing trip. I've let you rub your success in my face. I was stupid. I was hoping to someday build something like that of my own. But now . . . now that is all gone!"

"What are you talking about? You're jealous of my fishing success? Are you out there every morning fishing? Leaving everything you love at risk? No! Don't judge me!"

"I have nothing left! Your precious Joe took that away!"

"What?" Kira was surprised to hear his name come from Mrs. Perld's mouth.

Mrs. Perld was descending deeper into her personal hell. "Up north, your 'Joe' led his entire team into a trap. Everyone, including my Francis, died."

"What?" Kira's heart felt like it had dropped thirteen stories in an elevator.

"Yeah." Mrs. Perld was snarling now. "Everyone, except your precious Joe.

Kira felt her heart beating again. "Is he okay?"

"Get off my fucking boat!" Mrs. Perld screamed.

"Wait, you said he's alive. Does that mean he's okay?" Kira pleaded for information.

"Get off my boat, and never come back!" Mrs. Perld slammed the door in Kira's face.

"Wait! Is he alive!" Kira yelled at the door. There would be no answer.

Kira shakily walked back to *La Vida Dulce*. She looked out toward the ocean. *We need to get out of here, or this place will claim everything I love. It's trying to take Joe. Next it will come for the kids. I can't let that happen.* Kira looked toward the front of the boat. She had been preparing for something. She hadn't been sure what for, but her intuition had been telling her Key West wouldn't last forever. Now she knew it was almost time.

The island and the assault up north were being supplied with oil from active rigs in the Gulf of Mexico. These rigs had been cleared of any infected and put into full operation, supplying tankers running nearly around the clock. These rigs held one of the two keys to their freedom. They needed the fuel to travel anywhere.

Now looking at the numerous barrels she had tied to the front of her boat and hearing of Joe's unit's destruction but his survival, she made a promise to herself. Kira had been hiding a significant amount of gold. Now it was time to spend it. And she felt for the first time, knowing how much almost losing him hurt, how important Joe was to her. She wanted to give him something, the greatest gift she could, a chance for his hopes to be realized. They were going to leave Key West and find a way to traverse the Atlantic and go in search of Joe's brother.

Word around Key West was that a flotilla had been established in the Mediterranean. Several aircraft carriers formed the center of a floating island of ships and subsequent rings of smaller ships docked side by side. The result was supposed to be a city on the water. They were calling it "Newlantis."

Now she just needed the fuel, and Joe. She turned and went inside, but not before catching a scowling look from the boat across the back deck.

A set of eyes peered through pulled-down curtains. They were full of judgment. A neighbor had been listening to the fight. Kira glared back at them, hard. The blinds snapped shut. *Fucking coward.* Her focus and laser stare were so intense as she lasered that window with her glare that she didn't notice the sound of a passing gull complaining to the world about the lack of food, and she didn't notice the man watching her from a few boats down.

Chester Almont stood on the back deck of a smaller yacht just four boats down the row from *La Vida Dulce.* He puffed on a cigar and watched as Kira reentered her boat after a heated conversation with her neighbor. A crooked smile outlined his face. His plan was working perfectly. He could almost feel the jealousy in the air. The yachts were rife with it.

Over the last two weeks, he had been sowing seeds of dissent, and he had found fertile ground. The people here had lost much and had weakened resolve. This left an open door for his forked tongue. Every person felt guilt for his or her current situation. Survivor's remorse is what they called it. They were being weighed down by guilt like a boat held by an anchor. At this point, they were looking for anything to blame. Chester gave them that something.

First Chester began talking with the people who had lost children. He had approached them, asking simple questions about this or that. Then after talking with them for a while, he would say he had seen small children at the store the other day. The boater would say something along the lines of, "Oh yeah, those are Kira's kids. Well not really her kids, but she takes care of them." Then he would reply with a loaded statement such as, "Kinda makes you think back on your kids, huh? Like, why did they die and leave you childless while this young girl who didn't even want a family, had never loved someone like that, inherits three little kids. She is literally gifted a family while others have them ripped away. It doesn't seem fair." In the emotional state of many of these mothers, it hit home deeply in their subconscious. Only a few days later, they could not listen to or see the children playing. It became physically painful.

Next Chester went after the people who were struggling, barely getting by with their fuel allotment. He would time his conversations with these poor souls perfectly. He made sure to be talking to them when Kira came back from fishing trips. He would sow his seed with a statement as simple as, "Wow she has a lot of extra fuel today." Sometimes if he felt that it hadn't taken root in his target's mind, he would laugh and tell a story of her generosity for sharing fuel with other fishermen. Then he would say, in an aloof manner, "Well you know what I'm talking about?" The boat owner would reply, "No." Chester would respond in surprise and shock, "Really? Wait she doesn't share with you? Wow, sorry, my bad. I just figured, I mean, she has so much extra fuel and money that I just thought she would help people out. She helps out fishermen, so I guess I assumed she helped out her row." It only took a few good rumors to set a wildfire through the group.

The last boat owner that Chester needed to turn into an uncaring person, in order to execute his plan, was one he could not reach. She had family fighting alongside Kira's companion up north. Her loyalty to Kira ran deep. Chester took another long draw on his cigar. Fate, it seemed, had intervened on his behalf. News of the death of Mr. Perld and the survival of Joe were all that he needed.

Chester Almont had turned the world against Kira. Tonight Kira would find out why. Chester stood and walked away, down the ship deck. *See you soon, Kira.*

The sun had set about an hour ago. Chester munched on a bag of chips. From his surveillance position, he watched as Kira served dinner and read a story to the three small children. Jack and Elizabeth had fallen asleep during the story. Kira carried them to bed, followed by Christine. A few minutes later, Kira returned to the main deck to clean up. She really was a good mother. Chester thought back to the wife and

young son he had lost to a car accident about a year
ago. A sense of gratitude overcame him. He was
thankful they hadn't seen this zombie world. He was
even more thankful they wouldn't witness what he
was about to do.

Kira put away the last of the dishes from
tonight's dinner. The plate was part of a matching set
and fit neatly in a hideaway drawer. This boat had
been really well designed. She was wiping off the table
when a knocking at the back door made her jump. It
was late, and no one had come over in days.

Outside the door was a man she had never seen
before. He was about forty years of age, large, wearing
a T-shirt and overalls. On his face was a smile, and he
waved welcomingly. Kira returned his look with one
of a puzzled demeanor. Who was this guy? She walked
over and opened the door.

"Hello. Can I help you?" Kira asked.

"I certainly hope so." Chester nodded his head
in an appreciative manner. "I was actually hoping we
could help each other out."

"Okay." Kira was still very confused.

Chester looked around at the other yachts.
"Well it's something that can't be discussed in the
view of prying eyes. Can I come in?"

Kira thought for a moment. As she looked around, she spotted a set of blinds moving. She stepped backward, waving him inside.

Chester smiled and walked in. His plan had worked perfectly. Kira had grown suspicious of her neighbors. Her paranoia gave him his opportunity.

Kira closed the door behind them and pushed a button, closing all the blinds around the ship.

"So what did you want to discuss, Mister . . ."

"Almont, Chester Almont."

"Nice to meet you."

"You as well, Kira," Chester said with an excited tone.

Kira instantly furled her brow and grew suspicious. "How do you know my name?"

"Oh, I'm a fisherman, and I deal with Frannie. I've seen you talking to her a few times." Chester didn't really deal with Frannie. He actually resented her. She was what was called a "freshwater conch." People born in Key West proudly called themselves "conchs," while anyone who relocated to the area after seven years could be known as a "freshwater conch." Frannie had set up shop in town years ago, and her success had bankrupted two stores that were owned by born "conchs." But Chester was not against dropping her name in a ploy to gain some report with Kira. It worked. Kira shoulders eased, and her posture became less tense.

"Oh, okay. Well then, you said we could help each other out, how?" Kira asked.

"Well we are both fisherman, and it has not gone unnoticed that you seem to bring in a massive haul every day."

Kira sat down. "And?"

"And you have a very small boat."

Kira looked around the Marquis quizzically.

"A small fishing boat, I mean." Chester laughed. "No, your home is quite nice."

"Thanks. As for the fishing boat, it suits me fine."

"Yes, but it doesn't hold much of a catch. What I want to do is offer you an opportunity, one that you really can't say no to. I have a larger fishing boat with a much larger hold. You clearly have some sort of knowledge about where the fish are. So what I'm suggesting is that we team up. My boat, your fishing spots, together we can make a lot of money."

Kira thought for a moment. A larger source of income made sense. But something did not. Her intuition, or gut feeling, was saying no. She thought back to the last fishing team she had been a part of. How she had killed the man and taken his notebook. Did this man have the same plan? Was he really after the book? Would he kill her and take it? "I'll have to think about it." Kira stood and started walking to the door.

Chester reached out and grabbed her arm. "Wait."

Kira tried to pull free of the man's grasp but could not. "Let go of my arm."

Chester let go. "Sorry. Please. I need this. I've been having struggles. If I don't get a big catch soon, I'm going to have real problems."

"I think you should go."

"I can't. I need to catch fish. Look, I'm not catching enough. I'm barely getting enough fuel these days to run my big boat. You don't use much fuel, but my boat does. You have to help me."

"I said you need to go." Kira reached to open the back door.

Chester slammed his hand into the glass. He spoke through clenched jaws. "You're making this very difficult for me. I need this help."

"Get out of my house," Kira said with fierce determination.

"You're seriously not going to team up with me?"

"I'm not going fishing with you. We are not a team."

Chester grabbed her arm and pulled her close. He held hard, attempting to intimidate her. "Then give me the notebook."

"I knew it! That's all you wanted me for! Well you aren't getting it!" Kira said, determined and full of fury. Kira ripped her arm from Chester's grasp.

Chester slapped her hard across the face, sending Kira to the ground and stars into her eyes.

"Why do you need to make this so hard? Just give me the notebook and I'll be off. It's as simple as that," Chester said.

"Never." Kira scowled at Chester.

"See now, little lady, you're starting to make me angry. Give me the book and no one gets hurt."

"I won't give you anything! You piece of shit!"

Chester grabbed her off the ground, swinging her and throwing her hard onto the couch.

Kira let out a gasp as she slammed into the couch. Her eyes and nostrils flared as an angry, wild feeling started to overtake her. She was not backing down.

Chester noticed. "Tough one, are you? I wonder how thick your skin is if we were to involve the little ones." He pointed down the stairs.

Kira's eyes grew wide as shock surged through her body.

"Now you get it. So where is the notebook?"

She was frozen with some emotion she hadn't ever felt before. It was a need to protect, unconcerned for her own life all of a sudden.

"Fine. I'll wake the little ones up." Chester took one step toward the stairs.

Kira reacted. No one was going anywhere near her kids. She let out a scream as she jumped up from the ground and onto Chester's back. Kira was a wild animal, biting and scratching at any exposed skin she could find. Chester threw her off and grabbed at his bloody ear. His face was a series of bloody lines from Kira's fingernails.

Kira was now standing between Chester and the stairs going down to the bottom deck of the boat. Chester winced in pain as he touched his ear again. "You bitch!"

"Stay away from my kids!"

Chester began breathing faster, his sea-strong chest heaving as his face turned red with wrathful anger.

Kira attacked. She flung her whole mass at Chester. This time, she didn't have the benefit of surprise.

Chester caught her in his big hands and threw her down on the couch. He was on top of her, holding her arms down in a flash. "Where is it?!"

Kira responded with a well-placed spit in Chester's eyes.

Chester's face turned red as blood vessels popped, and any string of tenuous restraint snapped. He moved his hands from her arms up to her throat. He began squeezing with all his might. Kira felt the life being pushed from her. She felt blood rush to her eyes, and her vision began to blur. Stars and blackness mixed in the corners of Kira's eyes.

"I can find it even if you're dead. I know it's here somewhere."

As her life drained away, she didn't see a flashback of her life.

All she saw was Joe.

The Russian Wilderness:
Outbreak Day +66

Kurt woke and sat up straight with a massive amount of effort. He wiped the frost off his clothes and blinked the frozen sleep from his eyes. The icy cold of the Russian night had done everything it could to drain the last bit of warmth from Kurt as he slept. He cracked a crick out of his neck and absentmindedly stared at the hay-covered plywood floor.

The hunting blind had been a lifesaver when he found it last night. He needed shelter, somewhere his body heat would stay trapped. After climbing in, he had grabbed what pine branches he could to close up the door and other openings. Combined with some mud, that had been just enough to hold back the freezing night. Kurt stared at a beetle crawling across the ground. His body may be awake, but mentally he was still asleep. He had just had a great, and strange, dream.

He was trail running with his brother in South Florida. He could feel the heat on his shoulders and sweat pouring from his body as he raced Joe to the parking lot. It was heaven. Then at the end, Joe had been pulled from the dream, taken down a black hole, and disappeared. Panic had taken over Kurt as he tried to follow Joe. Before he could, his entire body froze. He could hardly move. Kurt looked down and saw himself trapped in an ice block. With all his mental strength, he fought the freeze as it enveloped his eyes. There was a moment where he almost gave up trying to open his eyelids again. The ice had too tight a hold, but he didn't. He kept fighting and eventually woke up in the hunting blind.

What did this all mean?

Was Joe gone? Had he lost him? He refused to accept it. He must be alive. It was that thought that had given him the strength to keep fighting as he froze. It was the belief his brother was alive that allowed him to wake up. Kurt clenched his hands into fists and released them. They were a purplish blue color. After about a minute, the color began to return. The whole time, Kurt thought, *wow, I almost died last night. I need to find better shelter and a fire soon or it won't matter.*

After a few more minutes of some light exercises to force his blood to flow, Kurt pushed the branches aside. It was still early morning. The sun fought against the frosty dew of the end of winter, trying to hold onto its chill. It looked like the air itself was only a degree away from freezing solid. He climbed out of the blind and onto the forest floor. His feet crunched through the frozen mud that had turned into icy tundra overnight. He persevered through the trees. Even as the ground turned back to mud after a few hours and his progress slowed, as Kurt had to constantly pull his foot out of deep mud, he kept pushing. Kurt was determined to get out of this muck and find some sort of civilization by nightfall.

The sun was getting close to setting as Kurt crouched by the edge of the tree line. He watched as his breath formed small spouts of smoky air. The temperature was already beginning to drop. Kurt had been hoofing it through the dense trees all day. His throat was parched, and his stomach was grumbling. He needed food, water and shelter, and he was staring at all three.

Kurt was looking out across an open field at a Russian military installation. It appeared to be a smaller base with only a few concrete buildings, several bunkers and a very large satellite dish. The outside of the base was lined with chain-link fences and barbed wire. Outside the fence was open ground with one sign. Kurt couldn't read Russian, but he knew what it stood for: a skull and crossbones in white paint emblazoned on a red sign, with Russian letters and an explosion graphic below it. Kurt's eyes followed the fence line until he spotted a gate. From the gate, a road led into the woods to his left. Kurt skirted until he reached the road. It was a rather thin two-lane road. Kurt had doubts. He could see obvious signs of zombie attacks. There were blood trails, spent ammunition and body parts lying around.

Kurt sat thinking about what to do next and saw a light appear in the window of the small, square building next to the satellite dish. He couldn't see anyone inside, but it looked like a glinting fire. The light was definitely flickering. Kurt felt his heart skip a beat. Someone could be alive. He had to risk it.

Kurt slowly worked his way through the damaged gate and up the long street into the compound. He crept along the side of buildings and through shadows of the fading light until he was next to his target building. He risked peering into the window. He couldn't see anyone inside, but he could see the fire. It was clearly a man-made fire. A small teepee of sticks burned and gave off white smoke, which pooled around the ceiling. The smell of burning pine filled Kurt's nose. Another pile of wood sat close to the blaze, waiting its turn in the fire. The small crackle of the fire could be heard. It made Kurt deaf to his surroundings.

Behind him, Kurt heard a gun cock. A cold shiver ran up his spine. The barrel of a pistol was pressed to the back of his neck. That shiver now spread throughout his body.

Kurt swallowed hard and forced out a weak plea. "Don't shoot. I . . . I don't mean any harm. I just saw the fire and—"

"Kurt?"

Kurt slowly turned his head around as the gun was pulled from his neck. Behind him, a young man stood holding a handgun. It was Tyler.

Kurt felt his shoulders relax. He grabbed Tyler in a strong hug. He looked at the face of his friend.

"Tyler! You made it! I thought you were a goner."

"Not yet." Tyler laughed.

"That's great! Where's Liz? Is she here too?" Kurt asked, looking over Tyler's shoulder.

"No. She . . . well she didn't . . ."

"Oh."

"Yeah. Well this is a messed-up world, huh?"

"Yeah."

"Well you better come inside. It's gonna get cold soon."

Kurt looked around at the ghost town of the compound. "Is it safe here?"

"I stayed here last night, and I'm still alive. So yeah, maybe. Come on, follow me."

Tyler led Kurt around the corner to where a steel door lay open. They stepped through, and Tyler secured a large deadbolt. Inside, a wall of warmth hit Kurt in the face. The small fire's heat was trapped in

the room nearly perfectly. The smell reminded Kurt of
the last time he had gone camping. Around the room
were scattered canteens and meal rations. The back
wall was a giant circuit-board computer connected to
the satellite. Its switches and dials all glowed red in the
dark space.

Tyler walked past Kurt and put one of the extra
pieces of wood onto the fire. "Welcome to my new
home. It's warm, not super comfy, and the only thing
to sleep on are some mats I pulled over from the
barracks. But it is secure. The door locks from inside
with a big metal lever and is the only way in or out.
The only catch is, I have to vent smoke after a few
hours or we'll get choked to death. I had to keep
opening it last night, and every time I did, I was afraid
the light would attract some unwanted attention. But I
haven't seen any yet."

"It's nice. Way better than where I stayed last
night. Does this place still have power?"

"It does now. Today after waking up, I
scavenged the camp. Found the food and water first,
and then found the camp's generators. Luckily
enough, they had been shut down with fuel remaining.
So I just started them back up. Then I came back and
found you."

"What is this place?"

"Well from what I saw today, I would have to
guess a missile base."

"A what?"

"Yeah, I know, right? Not too long ago, this
place was probably aiming at DC. Now it's just

nothing but some buildings. The underground silos are to the east."

"Wow."

"Yeah, on the bright side, I think that with this dish and the broken sat phone, I may be able to make a phone call home." Tyler held up the satellite phone, smiling. It had wires hanging from where the antenna used to be.

"Really?" Kurt's eyes grew wide with hope. He knew Joe never went anywhere without his satellite phone. If he was alive, Joe was only a phone call away.

"Yeah." Tyler bobbed his head up and down, and smiled. "No promises though. Remember, the main issue was that the antenna was fried. Well this building is connected to that massive satellite dish. Damn good antenna. If I can figure out what wires go where, I might be able to connect the phone to it. It's not going to be easy with everything in Russian, but I have hopes."

"Well that would be nice," Kurt said.

"No joke, right! Figure out if anyone else is still alive out there," Tyler said.

Kurt looked lustfully at the canteen pile. "Can I grab some water?"

"Of course. Are you hungry?"

"Absolutely."

"Here." Tyler grabbed a meal box and threw it to Kurt. "They taste terrible, but they'll keep your stomach from eating through your skin."

Kurt dug into his prepackaged meal, taking sips of water, as Tyler went to work on rewiring the input into the satellite dish. After a few hours, both men turned in for the night.

The Russian Military Outpost: Outbreak Day +67

The early morning light was beaming through the bulletproof glass windows as Kurt rolled up to a seated position. The last coals of the fire were dying. Tyler was deep into his wiring job. He heard Kurt stretching his body awake.

"How did you sleep?"

Kurt had slept better than he had in some time. "Amazing. It's a lot easier to sleep well when you aren't frozen."

Tyler laughed. "I'm sure that's true."

Kurt looked at his watch. 05:00. "How long have you been awake?"

Tyler responded, "This time? About an hour."

"This time?"

"Yeah. Woke up every few hours to vent the smoke, remember?"

"Oh, sorry. I should have helped."

"It's okay. I got you last night. Maybe tonight you help me."

Kurt looked out the window, staring at the trees. "You know we can't stay here."

Tyler didn't stop what he was doing. "I know. Trust me, I know."

Kurt turned toward Tyler. "What do you mean?"

"Well it's like you said before. In this world, if we stop moving, we're dead. I didn't believe you before, and look where that left us. We're stuck in Russia without a vehicle or soft beds, just trying to survive."

Kurt looked at Tyler's back. "And Liz would still be alive."

Tyler flinched. "Yeah, that too."

"What happened back there?" Kurt asked.

Tyler put down his screwdriver. He still looked at the wall of dials.

"Liz saved me. After you got cut off from us, Liz and I continued trying to reach the RV. There were too many of them. We didn't stand a chance. A group of zombies popped up right in our way. Toward the forest, there was only one zombie. Liz looked at me and told me she loved me. Before I knew what was going on, she took off in a full sprint and tackled the zombie. She screamed and yelled to me."

"For help?"

"No. She yelled, 'I love you. I did.' I took off into the forest and never looked back. I could still hear gunshots and people fighting, but I never looked back. I just put one foot in front of the other. I saw this base and ran to this room. I ran right through that minefield out there. I didn't realize it until yesterday. Do you know what that means?"

"What?"

"It wasn't my time." Tyler picked his screwdriver back up and started working again.

Kurt walked to the side of Tyler. "It's not your fault, man. She sacrificed herself for you."

"I know."

"Are you all ri—"

"Just let me work. Let's just get home. Let's just get the hell out of Russia."

"Okay."

A few awkward hours later, Tyler put down his tools and spoke animatedly. "I got it!"

Kurt looked up from a piece of string he was playing with. "What?"

"I got it! I have a connection!"

Kurt jumped up and ran across the room. He hovered over Tyler's shoulder.

Tyler looked at the jerry-rigged cell phone in his hands. He pressed the numbers in and put the phone on speaker. "It's ringing!" He and Kurt shared a moment of elation.

On the third ring, a voice came through. "Hello?"

"Dad?"

"Tyler?"

Tyler began to cry tears of joy. "Yeah, Dad, it's me."

Kurt could hear an explosion of happy cheering erupt from the cell phone.

"Dad, who all's there with you?"

"Everyone, son, we're all okay. The military rescued us."

"Thank God."

Liz's mom was speaking. "Is Liz there with you?"

Tyler looked up at Kurt. He had hurt in his eyes. Tyler switched the phone off speaker. Kurt stepped away to give him some semblance of privacy. Kurt walked to the window and looked outside again. The entire world looked like a different place. It was beautiful again. The pine trees waved in the wind, and the sun shined brightly.

A few minutes later, Tyler hung up his call. Kurt came over. Tyler was a mixture of relief and guilt.

"Are you all right?" Kurt asked.

"Yeah." Tyler wiped a tear from his cheek. "Want to try calling someone?" He smiled coyly.

"Oh yeah."

Kurt took the satellite phone and punched in the number for Joe's satellite phone. It rang once, then again and again. After six rings, Kurt's heart was dropping. On the seventh ring, it went to voicemail. Kurt wondered if his mind was just going into shock. He couldn't think of anything to say. He had been expecting him to answer. He had planned out a wonderful conversation full of love and "I miss you." Instead it was just a voicemail. Kurt said the first thing that came to mind and hung up. "314."

Kurt looked at the wall of dials.

"Sorry, man," Tyler said. "Kurt?" he asked. "Kurt?"

"We need to go." Kurt took a step out the door.

"Kurt," Tyler said with a sympathetic tone.

Kurt yelled back at Tyler, "What?"

"Kurt. I'm sorry, man."

"He didn't answer, so what? We need to get to him."

"Kurt."

"What? Why do you keep saying my name?"

"Man, you know what that probably means."

"No, fuck you. He just didn't have his phone on him. Maybe he is in the bathroom."

"In the bathroom?" Tyler asked kindly.

"It's possible."

"Maybe," Tyler said, with little belief in his voice.

"What do you mean 'maybe'?"

"Maybe it's better to let go."

"Let go?" Kurt was hurt by the thought.

"It might be easier to just not worry about him. It might be better to let go for now. Maybe you should accept he's gone."

"No. No. No! No! No, you're wrong!" Kurt was a mixture of anger and a growing feeling of despair.

"Kurt."

"You are wrong. You have to be wrong. You have to be!" Kurt fell to his knees. Tears began to run down his face. He put his head in his hands and sobbed. "You have to be."

After five hours of being inconsolable, Kurt now sat against a wall, a complete shell of a man. He stared absentmindedly at the cement floor. His mind was in a void somewhere.

Tyler sat against the opposite wall, munching on a meal bar. Tyler handed Kurt a canteen of water. Kurt took the water and sipped down a large gulp.

Tyler took the opportunity to start conversation up again. "I set the satellite phone up to be sending out a signal. Maybe it will get someone's attention. If someone's listening."

Kurt didn't respond. He didn't care.

Tyler continued. "I used your message to your brother. The signal is three beeps, a pause, one beep, a pause, four beeps, and a pause, on a loop. I know it's not much of a tribute to him, but I figured it's something. Maybe his memory will save us."

Tyler changed the subject. "My dad says that there are pockets of the US that are still alive. He says the military is fighting back against this zombie plague. It sounded like they were gaining ground."

Kurt was in a bad mood. The last real hope he held onto had just been ripped away from him. "So?" Kurt snipped back.

"So it sounds like there is still hope. There is still a world to return to out there. Humanity still exists."

"I don't care."

"Look, I know right now you don't care about anything, but you need to accept that the world isn't all bad. Sure, the zombies have robbed us of nearly everything, but we have a chance. If we make it out of here, we could go back to a normal life. No more running, no more watching people we love getting ripped apart. We can start over."

"I don't want to start over."

"You want to stay here? You want to live on the undead planet?"

"I don't want to live."

"Don't say that."

"Without my brother, I don't care."

"Don't you think he would have wanted you to fight on, to survive?"

Kurt looked up at Tyler.

Tyler continued. "I think he would have."

"Don't talk to me like you know what he would want. You don't understand. Your family is fine. They are living somewhere, happy and safe. I have lost everything! This evil world has taken it all from me! Don't talk to me like you have any idea!"

Tyler got angry. "Don't talk to me like I lost nothing! I lost Liz!"

Kurt got enraged. "Oh please! You aren't even broken up about that! I didn't see you shed a single tear for her!"

"You have no idea how much I have felt that loss!"

"Well it doesn't matter now, does it? You're alive, and your entire family is there waiting for you!

You get to go home and pretend that none of this happened! While I have to limp on in life without Joe! You don't know how lucky you are! Don't even try to compare yourself to me!"

Kurt and Tyler were screaming at the top of their lungs at this point. They were interrupted by the sound of a loud explosion. They both turned in time to witness a second and a third. Out in the minefield, dirt and body parts flew through the air.

A wall of zombies were working their way through, from the forest to the base. Hundreds of them were advancing. The screaming from their fight had attracted unwanted company. A fourth and a fifth explosion erupted. Bodies flew, and wails echoed through the air.

Tyler and Kurt looked at each other. They both read each other's mind: *Run.*

Tyler grabbed his gun. Kurt grabbed his pack. And they took off in the opposite direction from the minefield. They ran at a breakneck pace, only slowing to look over their shoulders. The zombies were making their way closer. The first of them had made it past the main gate and were on the way.

Kurt and Tyler covered the length of the base in a matter of minutes. They ran smack dab into a triple row of chain-link fence, about twelve feet high, rimmed with barbed wire along the top. On the other side of the fence was salvation.

The far end of the base backed up to a lake. In the middle of the lake was a small island with a pile of dead trees. The only thing that stood in the way was that fence. Kurt and Tyler started to climb, when they heard a noise they didn't expect: horns. Honking car horns were blaring from directly behind. They turned to see three RVs and a truck plowing through the zombie horde.

Kurt and Tyler jumped off the fence and out of the way just in time. The RVs and truck plowed through the fences right where they had been. As the vehicles screeched and ground against the chain-link and barbed wire, a large section was destroyed, giving direct access to the lake. A massive splash sent waves across the lake as the vehicles crashed into the water.

Kurt and Tyler chased after them. They dove into the water. In an instant, the breath was stolen from their chests. The water was ice cold. People came swimming out of the wreckage. They were survivors from the camp. Ten people had made it, including Jonathan and Brandon, the two brothers Kurt and Tyler had met weeks ago. Everyone began swimming to the island. Once they got there and pulled themselves from the frigid water, hugs were exchanged. Looking back, they saw a ring of zombies standing along the shore. They would not follow through the water.

The two brothers got straight to work. "Tyler, can you and Kurt get a fire going?"

"Uh, you wouldn't happen to have waterproof matches, would you?" Tyler asked.

"Here you go." Jonathan gave him a Zippo lighter.

"Thanks."

"Where are you guys going?" Kurt asked.

"We need to save what supplies we can," Brandon answered.

"You're going to swim back out there?"

"Look."

Kurt followed to where Brandon was pointing. Several coolers had floated to the surface.

"In those coolers are food and drinks. You guys get the fire going so we can get warm once we come back."

Tyler patted Kurt's shoulder. "Come on, Kurt. Let's go."

The sunlight was gone. Kurt and Tyler had made a giant fire. It was literally roaring as the dead trees first unfroze and then exploded into flames. Pitch-blackness consumed the world around the island. It was now an island in two ways. Not only was it land in the middle of water, but it was also light in pure dark, a flicker of brightness shining against the void. Even the shore was gone in the moonless night.

Brandon held up a bottle of wine. He and Jonathan had rescued four coolers from the lake before having to call it quits. Three of them were full of alcohol, and the fourth had an assortment of snack foods. All the survivors were sitting in a circle around a large bonfire. Brandon began his speech.

"First I would like to say that I know we've all been through a lot. We have been put through a literal hell, especially these past few days. We have lived in fear and have been chased like prey through the forest. We have all lost people, loved ones, family."

Brandon choked back his emotions and then continued.

"We have lost family, but we are not family-less. Look around you. This is your family now. Together we are one unit. Together is how we survive. The people around you are what drive you forward. They give you a reason to keep fighting. Even when we got ambushed and separated, it was our reuniting that kept us alive. Together, ten of us made it out of that camp, but we were lost. We didn't know where to go or what to do. We were stuck, surrounded on all sides by the zombies, and they were closing in. Low on gas, we didn't know what was going to happen next. Then a miracle happened. One whole section of zombies started leaving. We followed them, and where did they lead us? To Kurt and Tyler. We didn't know we still had family out there. They were still there and still alive. The zombies showed us the way to them. They are my brothers. Look, I'm not going to say we are in a great condition. That would be a lie. However, no matter what happens from here on out, we stick together as a family."

Brandon lifted his wine bottle high. "For those we have lost, and for the new family we have found."

He took a big swig from the bottle. Everyone in the group did the same with their drink of choice. Brandon had one last thing to say. "Let's celebrate one more night of life."

The group cheered. The drinks flowed like water, and everyone allowed himself or herself to let go, completely.

Kurt sat next to Tyler. "Tyler, look, about earlier . . ."

"It's okay, man."

"No it's not. I just lost my mind when I realized I was brotherless."

"Brandon's right, you aren't brotherless. You're my family now. You're my brother."

Kurt began to cry. Tyler hugged him. Tyler went back to the party. Kurt was too tired to drink; the emotion of the day had taken its toll. He fell asleep by the fire, leaning against a log, with the sound of laughter and revelry filling his ears.

Key West Harbor: Outbreak Day +68

Kira saw Joe a split second before she saw the glint of a combat knife sticking out of the throat of Chester Almont.

Joe had arrived home to find the large man trying to kill one of the people he loved. That was not going to happen. Joe dragged the limp form outside and threw him overboard.

Let the sharks take care of you.

He came back inside to find Kira sitting on the couch, staring at the small blood path Chester's body had left. Joe sat down next to her and put her head in his hands. He looked her over.

"Are you all right?"

She didn't reply, her throat still regaining its ability to move air.

"Kira, are you okay? Are you hurt?"

"I'm . . . I'm fine," she choked out.

Joe pulled her close and hugged her. The scent of his musk poured into Kira's nose. His warmth enveloped her. She sank into his embrace. As Joe pulled away, Kira took action.

She pulled him to her lips and kissed him.

Joe didn't pull away.

Chapter 4

The Russian Military Outpost Lake: Outbreak Day +68

The morning rays of sun penetrated through a dense fog that had settled over the small island. The survivors were all sprawled in a circle around the glowing embers from last night's fire. The warmth still held off the Russian, early-spring, icy dew.

Kurt rolled over and wiped water from his face. The ground had turned into mud. The permafrost had melted from the intense heat of the fire.

Kurt sat up and looked around. In front of him was the glowing fire pit. To his left was Tyler curled up in a ball, hugging a bottle of tequila. Kurt looked to his right. Brandon was sleeping, sitting against a log, an empty bottle of wine lazily leaning from his slouched hand. The rest of the group of survivors looked pretty much the same. Kurt stood and surveyed the aftermath of last night's party.

Kurt had fallen asleep and missed out on a rager. Empty bottles lay everywhere. There were bottles floating in the lake, lying spilled on the ground and sitting in the fire pit. Kurt worked his way to the coolers, doing his best not to step on a sleeping person or kick a bottle. He opened the coolers to find all the drinks gone. All that was left was a Capri Sun that had been skipped over. Kurt smiled.

He flashed back to playing soccer with Joe. Joe was a competitor. He wanted to win, and in most cases did. Kurt didn't care as much. He was just happy to be on the same team as Joe. Kurt's favorite part was after games. Someone would break out a container of cut oranges and pass around Capri Suns.

Kurt took the drink and pushed the straw through the puncture point. He accidentally pushed too hard, sending the straw out the back. Kurt looked at the Capri Sun, shaking his head and laughing under his breath. Soon he was full-blown laughing, his whole body shaking. *I can't even drink a Capri Sun right in this f-ing zombie apocalypse.*

After fixing the straw and drinking what he could, Kurt started walking around the island. He wanted to see what kind of supplies were close to shore that he could fish out.

Kurt looked out at the water. He could only see a few feet through this fog. He couldn't even see the short distance to the shore. A large bubble of air burst from the surface.

Must have been one of the car tires bursting. Kurt thought.

Kurt walked back to the camp. He climbed back up the muddy slope to where he had slept. He sat down and stared at the sky. A noise to his left caught his attention.

Tyler grunted as he sat up. "What the hell happened?

"Looks like you ate the worm."

"What?" Tyler was squinting and suffering a massive headache.

Kurt simply pointed at Tyler's hand.

Tyler hadn't even realized he was holding the bottle. He looked at it with disdain. With a heave, he threw the bottle into the fire coals. He put his face in both hands. "Ugh, I hate tequila. More specifically, I hate the morning after tequila."

Kurt laughed jovially.

Tyler leaned away from the noise. "Dude, do you have to laugh so loud?"

"Sorry."

"Some Advil didn't happen to float to the top, did it?"

"Sorry, bro."

"This world sucks."

"Yep."

"Is anyone else up?"

"Nope, you're the first."

"Why does my finger hurt?"

"Huh?" Kurt turned and looked. Tyler's finger was bruised and covered in mud. Kurt looked to where Tyler's hand had been. Kurt's boot print outlined exactly his handprint. *Oops.*

"Must have done something last night."

"Damn."

"Tyler, we're stuck here, man.

"What do you mean?

"I mean there is no more firewood and no way off this rock."

"Are the zombies still out there?" Tyler leaned to look at the far bank.

"I don't know. The fog is too thick."

"Just give it time. It'll burn off. It always does."

"I hope so.

"Well I'm going back to sleep. Wake me up if something happens."

"Will do."

Tyler lay back down to sleep off the hangover.

"Kurt, quit it, man."

"Quit what?" Kurt asked.

"Quit pounding your feet."

"I'm not."

"Dude, it's not funny. I feel terrible."

"I'm not doing anything."

"Look, I'm hungover, and I can feel those vibrations. You're going to make me sick."

"Vibrations?" Kurt lay down. He could feel them too. He stood up. "No way."

A scream cut through the air.

A face of torn and putrefying flesh was rising from the center of the fire pit. Its face caught fire and melted as the zombie continued to rise. Soon its arms breached the surface. Its whole body was in flames. Out of the fire pit poured the undead horde. It looked like an angry ant mound. They were climbing over each other and pushing through. Kurt's instincts took over. He slung his pack over his shoulder and grabbed Tyler, pulling and half-dragging him to a standing position. Tyler was half asleep until Kurt threw him in the water. The icy cold sobered him up in an instant.

He flailed and gagged. Only then did recognition dawn on him. He looked up at Kurt still standing on the shore.

"Kurt, come on!"

Kurt stared at the other survivors being swarmed. They didn't stand a chance. Even the few who had woken up at the sound of the scream couldn't run. They stumbled around, still drunk from last night's revelry. They were all too drunk or sick to stand a decent chance.

"Kurt, come on!"

The zombies had spotted Kurt. He took a step toward them, grabbing his backpack, and jumped into the water next to Tyler. Together they started swimming, not knowing what they would find on the opposite shore.

Key West Harbor: Outbreak Day +68

Joe squinted against the bright light shining in his eyes. The sun was pouring through the porthole skylight. It burned his retinas. He wouldn't be able to lie like this for much longer. It was torture, but he was too scared to move. Any slight disturbance could wake the sleeping beauty lying next to him.

Kira's arm was draped across his chest. Her hair rested across the pillow. Joe looked at her face. It was complete peace. Kira's eyelids flinched slightly as she dreamt. Joe looked at the curve of her nose and the

softness of her lips. He desperately wanted to kiss her.
The feel of their lips connecting had been almost
unbelievable. When their lips touched, he felt his legs
go weak and a tingle run through his spine. It had
been lightning in his soul. He felt temptation to kiss
her now, just to taste that feeling again.

What was he thinking? She had just kissed him
because she had been caught up in the emotions of
what happened the night before. Joe had been caught
up himself.

After saving her life, he couldn't bear the
thought of living without her. He hadn't pulled away
from her kiss. He had allowed his heart to open for
the first time since he had been in combat action.

Fighting overseas had made it much harder to
allow others to get close. He had lost many good
friends in the sands of the desert. One in particular
had taken its effect. It was his first tour. He had
become very close to a young private who reminded
him of Kurt. This man was optimistic and so happy. It
was like looking at his younger brother on Christmas
morning every day. Until one day, when Joe had to
watch as the man's Humvee was hit with a massive
IED. Some coward had planted the bomb in the
middle of Main Street. For the next few hours, Joe
had to pick up body parts with his men. One second
this great light was in the world; the next it wasn't.
The only thing to remember him by was bloody
pieces. It was too much. Joe had decided to go cold
from that day.

But here and now, something was different.
Kira was someone he felt responsible for. She was his
to protect. He had almost failed. It had been pure
good fortune that he had arrived home when he did.
Joe remembered the mess upstairs. He carefully slid
Kira's arm off him and slid out of bed. They had both
slept in their clothes. Last night, after sharing their
kiss, he and Kira had collapsed into the bed out of
pure exhaustion. Joe still hungered for what that kiss
promised. It would have to wait.

He went upstairs and began mopping up the
blood. As he finished, Joe went outside to dump out
the water. He looked around. Eyes stared at him
through blinds and tinted windows, the effect lessened
in the sun. He looked good and long at each of them.
Joe never broke his stare. Boat by boat, he won staring
contests. He didn't care if the other boats looked at
him like a murderer. As far as he was concerned, they
were all responsible for what had happened. Kira's
scream had reached Joe's ears when he was still down
the dock. He had sprinted down the boat decks to
reach her. What had they done? Nothing.

When Joe had last left, this had been a safe
area, where everyone was out on their decks talking
and playing with each other. What had happened?
This place was now a marina of judging and detesting
glances. It felt like an evil place. Joe tossed the last bit
of bloody, soapy water into the ocean and went back
inside. As he did, he heard small voices and steps
climbing up the stairs.

Jack's hair was sticking straight up on one side. His face was full of innocent joy. His eyes shined brightness and joy. "Mister Joe!" He ran to Joe.

Joe got down on a knee and gave the young boy a hug. "Hey, Jack. How are you?"

"Good. I'm glad you're home. I have to show you the playroom I made!

"You made a playroom? All by yourself?"

"Well Chrissy, Lizzie and Kira helped, but it was my idea.

"Was not!" Christine had come upstairs too. She was wearing a nightshirt and had her arms crossed in a full-body pout.

"Uh-huh!" Jack spat back at her.

Joe intervened. "Now I'm sure you both had a big part in making it.

Christine stuck her nose up with a loud, "Humph." She was satisfied that she had won the argument.

Joe held Jack's hand in his left and held his right out to Christine. "Do you guys want to show it to me?"

Christine grabbed his hand, a big smile on her face. "Come on!"

She led Joe and Jack down to the guest room. The third of the yacht's three bedrooms was now filled with colorful drawings, books, dolls and Legos. Jack and Christine took turns showing their favorite toys, sometimes forgetting to breathe.

Jack then asked the question he and Christine had been skirting around. "Will you play with us, Mister Joe?"

Joe answered, "Of course! I would love to play! But first, where's Elizabeth? Where's your sister?"

Christine answered, "She's scared."

"Why is she scared?" Joe felt his heart stop. Had the children seen what happened upstairs yesterday?

Christine continued. "She thinks you won't remember her."

A weight fell from Joe's heart. "Well that's crazy. Where is she?"

"She's with Miss Kira."

"Okay, guys, why don't you both pick something you want to play. I'm going to talk to Elizabeth, and when I get back, we are going to have some fun. Sound good?"

The children answered in unison. "Okay!"

Joe walked to the main cabin and opened the door slowly. Inside, Kira sat with Elizabeth in her lap. Joe entered the room. "Hello."

Elizabeth buried her face into Kira's stomach.

Kira started to talk. "Elizabe—" Joe stopped her.

"It's okay." Joe sat on the bed next to the two of them. "Hey, Elizabeth. I heard you were afraid that I might not remember you. I just wanted to let you know that was the farthest thing from being true." Elizabeth still didn't move. "Elizabeth, if you were away from your brother or sister for a while, you wouldn't forget them, would you?"

Elizabeth shook her head still buried in Kira's stomach.

"Well that's how I feel about you guys. When I was out there fighting, I thought about you a lot. I wanted to get back to see you. I missed you."

Elizabeth responded by releasing Kira and crawling over and hugging Joe. Joe hugged the little girl back. He looked up and made eye contact with Kira. Her eyes were wet with happy tears. Their little zombie-apocalypse-made family was back together.

The rest of the day was spent playing games and laughing. Joe and the three kids had tea parties, played hide-and-seek and even "taught" Kira how to play Go Fish. Christine insisted on teaching everyone.

That night, after putting the kids to bed, Kira and Joe sat out on the upper deck and shared a bottle of wine. She cuddled up to him as he put his arm around her.

"Kira."

"Yeah?"

"What happened around here? This place was nice."

"I don't know. I think people just got jealous. I mean, I have been fishing well and saving up money. Some people are barely getting by. I think they resent that fact."

"Are they having trouble with their fishing?"

"They aren't fishing."

"Oh."

"Yeah."

"Then what are they doing all day?"

"They aren't doing anything."

"Well no wonder they are struggling to get by."

"Well I think that most of these people had jobs doing stuff, and when the zombie thing happened, well those jobs just disappeared. They don't know what to do."

"They have to reinvent themselves. They can't just roll over and blame fate."

"It's not that easy, Joe."

"I know it's not easy, but it is possible. Look at you. You were a secretary at a yacht dealership. Now you're a fisherwoman who takes care of three kids, and you're strong." Kira smiled. Joe continued his adoration. "You are amazing. I can say that those kids and I are lucky to have met you."

Kira broke down. Tears poured down her cheeks. For a moment, Joe subconsciously patted himself on the back. He had made her so happy she was crying. The moment passed as Kira let out a soft wail and put her head in her hands, sobbing.

Joe pulled her in closer. "Kira, what's wrong?"

"He should have killed me," she choked out from a tear-filled throat.

"I'm here. I got here in time, and he won't hurt you again."

"No." Kira pushed out with a hint of despair in her voice. "He *should* have killed me. I deserved it."

"Don't say that. Don't let any of these people make you feel guilty because you are working."

"No. You don't understand."

"Kira."

"Joe, I killed a man."

Joe was slightly taken aback. "What?"

"I killed a man. I stabbed him and pushed him off the side of the boat."

"Another man came after you on the boat?"

"No." Kira's tears had slowed. Getting this off her chest was helping quell her emotions. "It's how I got the fishing boat."

"What?" Joe asked, completely confused.

"Well the second day we were here, I went out fishing, on that little boat." Kira looked over the railing at the boat. She kept staring at it as she told her story. "He, the man I went out there with, well he tried to rape me. And, well, I stabbed him and pushed him overboard. I watched as his body floated away and the blood pool spread. Then I . . . I just left him there. I came home and just lived on, like nothing happened. I never felt bad about doing any of it. I just accepted it and kept living, but this latest attack made me think. Is this karma? Am I just a bad person who deserves what's was coming to me? I mean, I literally took the murdered man's boat and notebook of fishing spots and have used it to profit, without ever feeling that bad about it. I only felt bad for basically that day, I guess. But after a shower, I was just okay. What kind of person does that make me?"

"It makes you a survivor," Joe said.

Kira still didn't look away from that boat. "I have blood on my hands. I killed him and stole the notebook, and here comes someone else who tries to do the same thing to me."

Joe turned Kira so that she was looking directly into his eyes. "Listen to me. You did nothing wrong. A man tried to rape you, and you fought back. That's all. You were able to provide for the kids downstairs. You've worked hard and done an amazing job. As far as karma or blood on your hands, no. Two men attacked you, and they got justice. In this world, this zombie-fucked-up place, not everyone is paying for their sins. Those men, they paid. One for his lust and the other for his greed, and envy. They got what they deserved. That's it."

"Thanks, I know you're right, but it doesn't feel that way," Kira said.

"I know, the first life you take always hits hard. But you've got to remember, it's true. It's rare for justice to happen these days. I," Joe paused for a second, "I'm the one who shouldn't be alive."

"Don't say that."

"It's true." Tears came to Joe's eyes. "I killed my whole team."

"Joe," Kira said sympathetically.

"I let my arrogance get in the way. I should have called the mission off. I was too full of myself, and we were slaughtered. We fell into a zombie trap. One that anyone would have seen a mile away. I didn't. I underestimated them on a morning that I was emotionally compromised from finding out my parents were gone. I made the mistake, and everyone else paid the price."

"Your parents?" Kira put her hands over her mouth.

"Yeah." Joe nodded his head. "I learned about it before the mission, and that clouded my judgment. I should have seen the mission parameters were wrong. I will carry that guilt for the rest of my life, and I don't know why, but God or destiny chose me to survive. Even in the hospital, a man, a brother of one of the soldiers I lost, came to kill me. He nearly succeeded, yet fate intervened again. I should be dead, but for some reason, I'm alive. The only thing that kept me here was pure luck, and a dream I had."

"A dream?"

"This might sound strange," Joe answered, "but you and Kurt saved me."

"What?"

"I saw you first in a dream I had after the man attacked me in the hospital. You made me promise to come home again. Then Kurt appeared. He said he needed me to save him. I saw the way he looked at me. I knew he needed me. He needs us."

Joe grabbed Kira's other hand. "Kira, I need to talk to you about something."

Kira could sense the fear in Joe's voice. He was afraid to say the next words, though she didn't know why.

"I received something. A gift," Joe said.

Kira sat silently.

"I was given great hope."

"Hope?"

"Yes. When I finally shook the effects of the painkiller the man tried using to overdose me, I had a voicemail on my phone."

"Kurt called you?" Kira asked, full of excitement.

"Yeah, he had called me and left a message. I don't know where he is or what's going on with him. There was a lot of static on the message, but I heard him clearly enough."

"What did he say?"

"Here. Listen." Joe pulled the phone out of his pocket, hit a few buttons and handed it to Kira. She put it to her ear and heard a faded voice say, "Three, one, four."

"I don't . . . I don't understand," Kira said, handing the phone back to Joe.

"Well when I was in Afghanistan, it was hard to communicate, so Kurt and I used a code from our childhood, 314, to let each other know we were okay. Sometimes I could only get online once every few weeks, so I would just send him a Facebook message with that, just to let him know I was okay."

"So that voicemail means Kurt's alive and safe?"

"As of a day ago, yeah." Joe was smiling from cheek to cheek.

"Wow," Kira said in a happy state of awe.

"Yeah, Kira, you remember what you said when we first got here, about what you'd do if your sister was still alive?

"Yeah."

"I have to go find my brother. A few days ago, when I was in the hospital, I heard this ringing. Now I was pretty drugged up at that point, so I thought it was my imagination. It wasn't. My satellite phone had been ringing. Kurt was calling me. He's still alive. I don't know how we are going to get there, but we can find a way. I'm sure some island nations are still alive out there. I have to go find him, Kira, but I can't go without you and the kids."

"Okay," Kira said, almost laughing with glee.

"Okay?" Joe asked, confused by how easy that sale was.

"Yeah, let's go find your brother," she said, smiling contently.

"Okay. Okay! We'll have to figure out how to get extra fuel and passage across the Atlantic."

"I might be able to help with that." Kira was having fun at this moment.

"How?" Joe asked, confused.

"Well over the past couple of months, I've been preparing for this." Kira laughed and smiled even wider. "I knew that I was doing it for a purpose, and just today I decided that going and finding Kurt was it. Of course, he called you a few days ago. Ha ha."

"Wait, really?" Joe asked, amazed.

"Yeah. I know you, Joe. You wouldn't leave people behind, especially your brother, after what happened with Aaron. I knew we had to find Kurt eventually, save what family we could. So I've learned the economy here. We fish for food just for the people here, but the oil rigs in the bay are still operating and shipping fuel to Miami. Then some of it is shipped to the Mediterranean to a floating island of ships much larger than here, which they call Newlantis. Well to make that journey, you need to carry fuel and pay the fee. Under that tarp up front are a bunch of oil barrels waiting to be filled, and I have saved up enough to fill them plus buy some rations for a long trip."

Joe was speechless.

"Well I knew how important your brother was to you, so I have been working on a way to go find him. Besides, you just said that he saved you, and you saved me, so I owe him too, I guess."

Joe jumped up and pumped his fist a couple of times. He could go after Kurt. "Oh my god. Oh, I love you!" Joe was pacing around the top deck.

Kira sat staring at him. Did he realize what he just said? He said it so casually. Was this for real?

"You love me?" she asked.

Joe froze. What he said had just connected in his mind. He had let the words just come out. Nothing felt wrong about them. He had seen Kira take care of the kids. He had seen the way she held silent strength and then melted in his arms, and he had felt her kiss. He turned and looked at her. This time, he took a serious tone.

"I love you."

Kira stood up and walked to Joe. He took her in his arms and kissed her. They melded into one. The warmth of her lips, the curve of her body, the hardness of his muscles, together they were perfect. Tomorrow they would get ready to leave and sail north, but now they let themselves be consumed with love.

Key West Harbor: Outbreak Day +69

The next morning, Joe was up early. He tied the small fishing boat and the kayak from Miami Beach, which had spent the last few months unused sitting on the fly deck, onto the back deck and sailed to the oil-drilling stations.

The *La Vida Dulce* headed south, out to the open water of the gulf. Its target was the nearest oil-drilling station. A few hours later, they neared the platform. A military fast boat came speeding out. The radio spat out angry commands. "Stop your engines or be fired upon!" Joe pulled back on the throttle. The Navy boat sailed a few circles around them for what seemed like an eternity and then swooped in quickly, coming alongside them. Joe stood on the back main deck to talk, with his arms raised.

A man on a bullhorn spoke over the short distance between the boats. Other men had rifles trained on Joe. "You have entered restricted waters! What's your purpose here?"

Kira sat inside, out of view. "Joe, that's not right. None of this is. There isn't supposed to be military here."

Joe spoke softly to her. "Most people don't know, but the military had to take a few over after some Enerjax outbreaks."

The Navy man was getting impatient. "What's your purpose here?" His speech was louder and angrier.

"We came to buy fuel," said Joe, clear and loud.

"This is military operation. Unless you're military, you need to leave."

Joe yelled back, "My name is Captain Joe Feller, search and rescue, New Florida Keys Army."

The Navy boat circled in closer so the two boats were nearly touching. "Holy shit. It really is you, Captain Feller."

Joe recognized the man instantly. "Good to see you, Petty Officer Kyle."

"You too, sir. I heard things. Heard about what happened and that you were done. Everyone says you're a cripple or that you mentally cracked."

"No, neither actually. While I was recovering, I received word that I have family alive. Combine that with the base commander changing tactics to a ground assault, bridge blitzkrieg strategy, and my skills aren't needed anymore. Plus they gave me their graces to head out, and an M4,"

"Yeah, commander also had no problem dumping all the blame on you and saying he kicked you out."

"Yeah." Joe gritted his teach a little.

"What did happen, sir?" Seaman Kyle asked.

"They're smarter than you think, Kyle. They can lay traps and have battle strategy. Accept that, and don't underestimate them. That's what we did."

"What does that mean? Are they still human?" Seaman Kyle asked.

"I don't know. Honestly, I don't care. Right now, I just need to find my brother."

"I wish you luck with that."

"Thanks, well we were hoping to purchase fuel." Joe waved to Kira, who came out holding Elizabeth, who had run up to her scared after hearing the bullhorn. They stepped out and stood next to Joe.

"I didn't know you had kids, sir."

"Well I do now. It's complicated. I guess everything in this zombie world is."

"That's true. But, sir, I'm sorry, we can't sell gas. Regulations sent down from command prohibit it."

"We have the barrels and gold, seaman, we need just to fill up before heading north."

"Are y'all going to New Miami?"

"That's the plan."

"You won't need to fill those barrels for that trip, sir, but you know that. Is that where you brother is?"

"No. He's across the Atlantic. We need the fuel to join the convoys."

"Oh, I see. But I still can't sell you any, sir. Even though down here, I'm technically the highest-ranking officer, I can't do that. Even if I wanted to, I have ten other men to think about, who would all get sent to a shitty post if we disobeyed command. You understand, right? Here we aren't battling zombies or dealing with the smoke and stench of burning bodies. The food sucks, just old MREs, but other than that, life is heaven here compared to the rescue missions."

Kira joined the conversation, yelling a question. "When was the last time you had fresh fish?"

Seaman Kyle laughed. "Probably over two months now. They don't send fish out here."

"How about you sell us the oil, and we give you something better than gold?"

"And what's that?" Seaman Kyle asked sarcastically.

Kira put Elizabeth down and ran inside. She quickly emerged holding up the notebook. "In this notebook are all the best fishing spots around here. I personally used this to accumulate all the gold and barrels we have. You can also have the small fishing boat tied on the wet deck and all the tackle we have. You and your men could have fresh meals from now on."

"Captain, be real here. Is she just talking shit? I'd love a good meal. So would the men. But how can we trust this? If it was anyone else, I wouldn't even be talking to them anymore," Seaman Kyle said.

"Come tie up to us," Joe invited. "I'll show you the proof."

The Navy boat pulled up. Seaman Kyle tossed a line across, and Joe quickly tied the vessels together. Seaman Kyle stepped onto *La Vida Dulce*. Joe first opened the storage area underneath a bench on the back deck, where life jackets would normally be kept. Instead was a haul of fish packed on ice. Joe next led Seaman Kyle to the bow and showed him the barrels. "See?"

"I see fish and barrels. How does that guarantee that you aren't lying?"

"Kira? How far away is the closest fishing spot?" Joe asked.

"With the fishing boat, probably thirty minutes. With that Navy ship, like fifteen."

"So you send some men to go fish that spot while we fill the barrels. If they find fish, then we give you the fishing ship and the notebook. If we are lying, you can just shoot us all."

"Joe!" Kira said, covering Elizabeth's ears.

"Or just cancel the deal," Joe said. "Well what do you say, Kyle? How about fresh fish for you and your men? Plus the rods, some tackle and bait to get you started. And you won't have to worry about shitty delivery schedules for food. I'm sure you've run short once or twice. Sounds like a good deal, right?"

"You realize you would be putting a target on your backs. The whole trade in New Miami runs on fuel. Being rich in fuel is dangerous," Seaman Kyle said.

Kira spoke up again. "I've got a plan for that."

Joe nodded toward Kira and turned back to Seaman Kyle. "So do we have a deal?"

Joe and Kira sat on the fly deck as they headed north, hugging the coast line. They were sailing full of fuel and light one fishing boat. Joe looked at the islands as they passed by. They had just stopped off at a small, uninhabited one for palm branches for Kira's plan.

"So now we've got the fuel, Kira." Joe looked at the barrels. He could barely see them under the tarp and palm branches that were piled on the side of them. "Are you sure about this ruse?"

"Listening to the chatter on the radio, New Miami has no need for water. So being so poor in fuel that we are collecting coconuts to avoid using the desalinating pump should help make us less of a target, hopefully. Plus I have been hanging the kids' drawings on the windows. I think people will assume that having other people to look out for makes it harder to be rich, or at least not rich enough that people will come after us."

"Let's just hope we don't get asked about it at all," Joe said, unsure. "Now how do we join one of these convoys you've heard of?"

Kira rubbed her face. "I'm not sure about that. I heard about all of this by sitting, listening to the radio, so I didn't exactly get all the details. From what I understand, they stage out of Miami Harbor, and I've heard them name the mayor, but I think we'll have to approach and ask the convoy ourselves. They seem to want all who want to come. The convoys are run for profit, so you pay and they accept you. I assume that would be simple. Plus since we wouldn't drain on their oil reserves, they should give us a discount."

"Why?" Joe asked.

Kira continued. "Well people pay for safe transport, but the main way they make money, according to the radio, is by selling oil along the trip and when they arrive at Newlantis. Newlantis somehow has manufacturing setup, I guess. I just heard that they can make ammunition, which we need to keep clearing the islands and regain ground. So it's pretty open trade."

"What else have you heard about Newlantis?"

"Not much. I did hear that they have mastered sea farming. There are rumors of fields of corn on ships. And that you get steak because some islands have been cleared, so they are growing livestock, but that sounds like it's too good to be true."

"Corn growing on a ship? That would be a sight to see."

"Yeah."

"Well I guess the first thing to do is find a convoy and join it. This should be fun."

The convoy was floating about twenty miles off Miami Beach. Joe had been on the radio as he approached and had been directed to pull up to and float near a deep-sea buoy. The convoy could be seen on the horizon. It looked like a small city floating on the sea.

The *La Vida Dulce* had been floating idly for about ten minutes when a go-fast boat came out of the middle of a small armada of ships. It coasted to a stop a short distance away. The radio came back to life.

"Name and boat name?"

"My name is Joe. This is *La Vida Dulce*. We are looking to join the convoy."

After a short pause, the man on the other end of the radio spoke back. "I don't have a 'vida dulce' or 'Joe' on my records. How long ago did you get mayoral approval?"

Joe responded, "We just came up from the base at Key West. We have plenty of—"

Joe was interrupted. "Hold up! Stop! Let me stop you right there. You must have mayoral approval to join this convoy."

Joe didn't want to deal with whatever New Miami was. "Look, we just want to join—"

The man interrupted again. "Not without mayor approval. You must go into New Miami and obtain the proper approval. Then you can join a convoy."

"What if—"

"No. Stop. There are no exceptions. You can't buy your way in. You must get approval. Then come back. Oh, and don't try without it. We have no problem sinking ships and sacrificing lives to maintain the convoy. Are we clear?"

"Okay, I understand. Calm your tits."

"Ha ha ha." Laughing came from the other side of the radio. "Did you just tell me to calm my tits? Ha Ha. I like you. What's your full name, Joe?"

"Joe Feller."

"Okay, Joe Feller, are you a doctor or anything like that? Something useful?

"I'm military."

"Okay, any leadership experience?"

It was Joe's turn to laugh. "Ha ha, some."

"Great. What was your highest rank?"

"I'm a captain."

"You *are* a captain? Going AWOL?"

"It's complicated." Joe wasn't amused at the implication.

"Well what isn't these days, right? Okay, hold on a second." About a minute passed before the man came back on the radio. "Well, Joe, it seems someone in New Miami has heard your name before. I guess you'll get your mayoral permission from the man himself. Do you have something to write down on?"

Joe grabbed a small stationery pad and a crayon the kids had been using. "Yeah."

"Okay, go into the harbor, up Government Cut, and go to where Bayside Marina used to be. You'll find the marina a lot larger with boats tied to each other in long docks. Go to the fifth from the right. There is an open mooring area there for short-term visitors. Go and tie up, and I'll make sure the right people come to you so you can meet the mayor. Oh, and a word of caution, don't trust anyone there. New Miami is a vile place. Unlike the convoy, it doesn't have a great system of rules. So be safe."

"Thanks."

"You're welcome, good luck. Remember, don't come back without mayoral approval."

Joe steered toward New Miami. "Miami, here we come. I did promise I'd be back."

The Russian Military Outpost Lake: Outbreak Day +68

Kurt and Tyler pulled their freezing, wet bodies from the Russian lake. They trudged up onto the muddy shore. Kurt was on his hands and knees, while Tyler had his hands interlaced on his head as he lay on the ground, staring at the sky. The short swim had been the most difficult of either of their lives. The icy lake had gotten colder. Moving around in those waters was painful. Every stroke felt like slamming their arms into a bed of sharp needles. The sounds of screaming from the island had stopped during their swim. Now it was silent, except for the noise of their heavy breathing.

Kurt looked around them in a full circle. There was no one around. The zombies had lost them. Kurt took a chance at talking to Tyler. He had to. His mind was running wild with a thought he needed to voice.

"They tunneled. They frickin' tunneled to us."

"What are you talking about?" Tyler asked.

"The zombies dug under the lake to reach us. They're smart. I mean, at least smart enough to find a way around the water."

"That's ridiculous."

"Is it?"

"Yes. Zombies are not smart. They are mindless creatures. You saw them running through that minefield. Remember when those things exploded?"

Kurt hadn't gotten that image out of his mind. "Yeah."

"Did you see what the others who hadn't gotten hit did?"

"No." Kurt had been too busy watching the pieces of the ones getting hit.

"Well they continued coming. There was no hesitation or worry. They didn't know what was going on."

"Or they were just too hungry to care. They took the risk. I mean, they have some level of intelligence. They didn't walk into the water."

"Yeah. Why is that?" Tyler asked.

"You've seen those things. There is no way they have enough coordination to swim."

"Can they drown then?

"I guess."

"No way, man, they came up from underground. There is no oxygen underground. I don't think they breathe."

"What then? Why are they afraid of it?"

"Beats me."

"Well they tunneled."

"Stop it."

"Look, man, I saw bubbles."

"Bubbles?"

"Yeah. I thought they were from a tire under the lake, but it could have been from a collapsing tunnel."

"Your whole argument is bubbles?"

"Well they got to us somehow."

"Yeah they did." Tyler rolled over, stood up and extended Kurt his hand. "Come on, man, let's get the hell out of here."

Kurt grabbed his hand and pulled himself up. The two started walking along the shore in the opposite direction of the spot where the vehicles had crashed into the lake yesterday.

The fog was starting to lift. A roaring sound was coming from up ahead. Kurt and Tyler inched forward slowly. The outlet from the lake was a ten-foot-high waterfall that fed a system of rapids and rushed downstream. The noise was near-deafening. Kurt and Joe relaxed slightly when they saw the raging river. Lying across the lake's outlet over the drop of the waterfall was a thick log.

Kurt turned, smiling, to look at Tyler, who was standing behind him. His smile was wiped away in an instant.

Twenty feet behind Tyler was a wall of zombies advancing at his back. The sound of the water had masked their approach. Tyler saw the fear in Kurt's face and turned instinctively. He saw the horde.

They both reacted by starting to cross the icy, slick log. It was about twelve feet in length. After covering about seven feet of it, Kurt saw zombies coming to the other side of the log as well. They were trapped. Kurt looked at Tyler. He was asking the same question in his mind as Kurt was: *What do we do now*

The zombies were mulling at both ends of the log. They were deciding what to do, just like Kurt and Tyler. Tyler took action. He slammed his boot into the log with all his strength. The log had been swollen and splintered from last night's freeze. The warming temperatures combined with the added weight broke the last straw, or in this case, log. With a loud snap, the bridge gave way, sending Kurt and Tyler into the icy, raging stream.

The icy water filled Kurt's mouth and lungs as he fought against the current. The frigid temperature pushed the breath out of his lungs. He threw tired, cold arms around, trying to swim. Rocks beat against his legs, bruising his shins and knees. He struggled with the rushing stream, fighting for every breath. Choking and spitting, he eventually found his way into an eddy that formed about two hundred feet down the river, behind a fallen tree.

Kurt dug his fingers into the river's bank. His nails scratched into the clay as he pulled chunks of mud from the bank. His feet dug deeply into the ground as he crawled free from the icy stream. He pulled his choking, shivering, shaking body into the forest. Kurt stood up on wobbly legs. He looked around, trying to assess his surroundings. Out of the corner of his eye, he saw Tyler. He was another twenty feet downstream. His body had been high-sided on a rock. It was sitting half-in and half-out of the water.

Kurt took off down the shore.

His feet and boots splashed as the water sprayed into the air from his jogging steps. He ran up to where Tyler was. He couldn't reach Tyler without getting back in the river. Kurt walked a few feet back upstream and jumped in. He planned it perfectly. The current pulled him right to Tyler. Kurt grabbed him. With the added momentum of Kurt's form, they pulled free from the rock. Together they flowed downriver. Kurt now fought the current and gravity, trying to keep both their heads above water. Forty yards downstream, the river turned and widened, giving Kurt the chance he needed. He swam to the opposite shore, one arm around Tyler, dragging him along. He pulled Tyler free of the water and put his ear to Tyler's mouth.

"Thank God you're still breathing." Kurt looked around. He heard nothing coming from the woods around them, but he did see signs of civilization. A river cabin sat thirty feet downstream. Kurt picked Tyler up, struggling under his weight. Kurt carried and dragged him the distance to the cabin.

Kurt set Tyler down behind a rock, leaning against it, and set out to explore the cabin. It was super small, only about ten feet long by six feet wide. A slim, metal chimney stuck out from one corner of the roof. There was one square window, if you could even call it that, on the side of the cabin and a simple door on the front that led onto a single stair.

Kurt circled around. The cabin on the other side was windowless but had a short canoe hanging on hooks. A few feet away from the cabin was a shed just as big as the cabin itself. A master lock held a latch in place. Next to the shed was a pile of chopped wood, neatly stacked. Kurt looked around and spotted a single outhouse about twenty feet into the woods, but nothing else.

Kurt went to the door of the cabin. It was locked, but with a small shove, it gave way. He slowly entered the cabin. "Hello?" No one was home. It was as simple on the inside as it was on the outside. A set of bunk beds with some blankets piled on them sat on one wall, with a small stove in the corner that was connected to the chimney. It was all cast iron, a classic wood-burning stove with a flat top for cooking. A pot sat on top of it. That's all that was inside. The only other thing was a key hanging on a hook just below the small window.

Kurt grabbed it and walked back to the shed. One twist of the key and Kurt unlatched the lock and stepped inside the shed. Inside were white buckets, all placed on shelves lining each wall. Boxes sat on the floor, piled to the roof. Kurt examined the closest bucket. It had Russian letters handwritten on it in black ink. He opened it. Kurt could cry. Inside was rice. Kurt opened another and found more rice. He next opened a box and found it to be packed with Russian MREs. There was enough food to last a while. Kurt turned to go back to Tyler and saw a medical kit on the back of the shed door. He grabbed it and headed for Tyler.

Kurt grabbed Tyler, carrying him inside, and plopped him down on the bottom bunk. He looked at Tyler's leg. A huge, open gash was still bleeding slowly. Kurt grabbed some gauze from the kit. He looked at Tyler. "Thank God you're not awake for this." Kurt roughly wiped the wound of dirt and dead skin. Next he poured some alcohol from the kit on it and wrapped it back up. Tyler was out cold, but he still moaned in his delirium.

Kurt talked to him as he pulled a blanket over Tyler's body. "Don't worry, man. You're going to be okay. I'm going to get a fire started and warm you up. I've still got the lighter from the bonfire, amazingly enough, and my backpack stayed attached to me even after that tumble in the river. Then I'll make some food. With the stores outside and my water-filtrating Nalgenes, we'll be able to stay here a while. What do you know? The backpack actually saves us after all. Don't worry. I got you, man. I got you."

Chapter 5

New Miami Harbor: Outbreak Day + 69
After explaining to the children what was
happening, Joe had asked Kira to keep them
downstairs with the blinds shut as they pulled into
Government Cut. He didn't know what to expect.
What he saw when they arrived was beyond his
wildest expectations.

Joe was standing on the fly deck as he sailed up
Government Cut. At first, upon seeing the seemingly
undamaged Portofino Tower, he had gained some
hope that maybe Miami and Miami Beach had held
together somehow. Maybe that convoy liaison had
exaggerated the situation to scare him. The tower
stood tall as ever, shining in the sun. The facades and
windows glinted brightly. It didn't seem like anything
was different. His gaze moved over to Fisher Island.
It, too, seemed untouched. The condos and
apartments sat quiet. The beaches were clear. Palm
trees swayed in the breeze. Then as he piloted the boat
farther into the harbor, the hope Joe had found
disappeared. His eyes had fallen on MacArthur
Causeway. This was not the happy vacation spot
Miami had once been. An undulating mass of bodies
wriggled for hundreds of yards, pressing into each

other, barely any air between them. The scene was enough to trigger a claustrophobic response in Joe's head. The mass of undead were all trying to press west, toward downtown Miami, but the road was blocked. Burnt-out vehicles and buses had been turned on their sides and piled high, forming a makeshift wall across the causeway.

Zombies were scratching, clawing and trying to climb the wall. On top stood men with metal poles. They were pushing the leading undead back down. One man waved a welcoming hello. Joe waved back. The man had a big grin on his face. He looked almost like a greeter at an amusement park. He was just so happy, too happy.

His smile finally steeled Joe's thoughts. *What a weird world this is.*

Joe piloted the boat into the bay near downtown Miami. It was exactly as the convoy envoy had told him. The makeshift boat docking formed a twisting and bending matrix of ships as the currents pulled them back and forth. It was like Key West, but bigger and less organized.

The city itself was a picture of the apocalypse. Buildings were toppled, and pieces of rubble crumbled from their structures. Others were untouched. It took Joe a moment to figure it out, and then he saw the pattern. The buildings had toppled over, creating a wall of cement and steel.

Joe could see glints of light reflecting off moving metal in the distance. *Must be more pokers like the smiling man on the causeway*, he thought to himself.

Joe studied the scene, and from what he could tell, the buildings had created a semicircle around the water, starting from the bayside park, reaching all the way north, just past the causeway. Joe smirked as he passed a double-sided road sign that was hanging from the bottom of the underpass of the causeway bridge. "Welcome to New" had been slathered in white paint next to the printed "Miami."

Joe couldn't help but read it out loud and laugh. "Welcome to New Miami." He added, "Hopefully we're welcome."

Joe found the open spot he had been directed to in the boat docking and pulled in. Kira tied it up to a barge that was acting like a makeshift dock. Joe rechecked the tarp. It was tied securely, and a few small pieces of palm leaves and a well-placed coconut could be seen poking from under the tarp.

After a few minutes docked, Joe had changed into his military gear. He wore his uniform pants, boots and blouse. He figured that if he looked military, it would carry more weight. At least people would know he wasn't weak. He holstered his sidearm and grabbed his rifle. It was an M4 he had taken from the base when he left. He slung the shoulder strap on and headed upstairs.

Kira was kneeling, talking to the kids.

"Okay, and remember what I said?" Kira asked the three children.

"Yes, Miss Kira. Don't open the door unless you use the special knock," Jack answered.

"And what is that knock?" Joe asked in a commanding tone.

The kids looked at him. They all had a little fear in their eyes. Joe was geared up and ready for action. His jaw was locked and his face hard. Jack practically whispered, "Three, one, four."

Joe nodded. "Good." He took a knee so his eyes were on the same level as theirs. "We should be back before night. If we aren't, you stay hidden here. I promise you, we will be back."

"What about Daddy?" Christine asked.

"What?" Joe said, caught slightly off guard, his hard face melting for a second.

"Well you said we'd come back for him. Is he going to come with us now?" she asked.

"I'm not sure." Joe hadn't realized that Kira hadn't yet explained that their dad wasn't coming back. "I'll ask the mayor and see if he's seen him."

"Can we come help you find him?" Jack asked happily.

"No!" Joe said rather harshly. "No matter what, do not leave this boat. Understood?"

All three nodded, too scared to talk.

"Now head downstairs."

The children followed each other silently in single file.

"You're scaring them." Kira was wrapping a scarf around her head in an effort to hide her face slightly.

"They should be scared, and you should too." Joe was all business.

"But, Joe . . ."

"No, no buts. We are about to go into a dangerous city. I know that it seems harsh, but they needed that right now. You need to be prepared too. You heard the warning from the convoy, right?"

"Yeah, I was listening to the radio call."

"Look, you're going to see things that I wish you didn't have to see. Don't react. No matter what you see or feel, just keep moving. Accomplish your goal, get the supplies we need and get out of there, back to the boat, as efficiently as possible."

"Okay," Kira said with a somewhat flippant tone. She didn't like being lectured.

"Seriously. No matter what, remember that what you see is normal life here. It's the status quo. You won't understand it, and it may seem wrong to you, but the people here live this way. Don't do anything to upset the system." Joe had flashbacks of Afghanistan for a second. He had seen men smoking and getting drugged up while the women worked. One time, a woman had looked at him and smiled. The next day, her husband had beaten her. When Joe saw her swollen face, he had wanted to go teach the husband a lesson, but he was the leader of the village. The Army needed their cooperation to save American lives from the Taliban. He wasn't allowed to risk that for anything.

Kira's confused and concerned tone in her next sentence broke his flashback. "Wait, aren't WE getting the supplies? You'll be with me the whole time?"

"No. There isn't time."

Kira looked at Joe, suddenly more nervous.

"Take this." Joe handed Kira the KA-BAR combat knife. She looked up at him. He responded, "Just in case."

Kira nodded, centering her strength.

The pair walked out of the yacht only to be greeted by three men carrying assault weapons.

Joe stepped in front of Kira, shielding her. The man in the middle lowered his rifle. The other men remained trained on Joe. The man in the middle spoke. He was tall and of average build. He wore a white business suit a size too small and stained. Around his neck hung a thick gold chain. He looked like a cartoon.

"Are you Bob?" the man asked.

"No," answered Joe, clear and strong.

The man paused for a moment, looking Joe over. He asked, "Are you Joe Berger?"

"I'm Captain Joe Feller. I'm expected."

The man smiled. "Well I guess you're the man I'm supposed to meet then. I'm Raul." He turned and nodded to the two other men. They lowered their rifles. Turning back to Joe, Raul spoke in a relaxed manner. "I'm going to escort you to the mayor's office, but first, there's the little problem of paying the docking fee. It's a gram of gold or two of silver to dock for each night. Double that for protection."

Joe knew protection schemes well. Either you pay or these men would rob you and destroy your belongings. He didn't have much of a choice. Joe reached into his pocket and grabbed out a gold ring that had been used as trading currency in Key West. He held it up to Raul. "This should be about right."

Raul reached out and took it. He placed it in his palm, feeling its weight. Nodding, he placed the ring in his suit pocket and turned to his men, giving them a thumbs up. They walked off, presumably to patrol the harbor. Their protection scheme only worked if other thieves didn't encroach on their territory.

Raul turned back to Joe and Kira. She had stepped around Joe and now stood next to him. Raul leaned his head to the side, like a lizard twisting its neck, hungry for a meal. "Is she yours?"

Kira took offense at the question. "I'm not anybody's. I'm not something that can be owned." Kira glared at Raul.

Raul's eyes moved up and down Kira's frame, eventually meeting her stare after a long survey. After a few moments, he straightened his neck and turned to Joe. "Better watch that one," he said in a playful tone.

"She'll be fine," Joe said back, strongly.

Raul shrugged, laughing. "Follow me and I'll take you to the mayor." He turned and walked down the dock.

Joe and Kira followed.

A few minutes later and Joe, Kira and Raul were walking along a side street. Raul was acting like a tour guide. He pointed out buildings used for entertainment, trading and companionship, all of which were less than welcoming. They came upon what used to be the American Airlines Arena. It had tents on the steps leading into the arena, and the door and windows were blown out.

"Here we have the market. Buy anything you want. From pieces of normality to zombie art."

"Zombie art?" Kira asked.

"Yes, we have some talented bone sculptors and inscribers," Raul answered.

Kira wrinkled her face in distaste.

"Hold on a second," Joe said.

Joe spoke quietly to Kira as Raul tasted a sample of roast squirrel being sold at a stand.

"Okay, listen, take the silver, buy what we need and get back to the ship. Oh, and remember, whatever you see that is wrong, it's not wrong here."

"Yeah, I got it. I'll be fine."

"I know. I love you."

"I love you too."

Joe and Kira kissed. She walked up the stairs heading inside.

"She decided she wanted to go shopping, huh?" Raul sidled up to Joe, watching her from behind. "Women, some things never change."

Joe shot Raul a glance.

Raul shrugged and continued forward. Joe took one last look at Kira and followed Raul.

New Miami Market: Outbreak Day +69

Kira walked up the stairs to the American Airlines Arena. All the glass was broken on the main level. Colorful sheets blew out of them in the wind. Those that used to welcome people to the arena had been ripped off their hinges. Yet other than that, nothing on the outside seemed to be damaged. The multiple-story front wall made of glass was mostly unbroken, just a slight covering of dust.

A pair of women wearing coverings over their faces came out the door. Each reached a hand to her forehead, shielding her eyes from the sun, passing Kira as she surmounted the final few stairs. The first thing that hit Kira like a sweet wave was the smell of baking bread. It made her stomach growl instantly.

Kira moved with a little extra pep in her step as she went inside. She took a moment and gazed around the main entry area. The front wall of glass let the sun in, illuminating a colorful world of booths spread out across the entire lobby. Most of them were square EZ-UPs, set up so vendors could pitch their wares.

Kira walked by a man selling fabrics, another selling palm-weaved mats and another selling perfumes. She kept pushing deeper into the market, following her nose, suddenly in search of bread. A short distance down the concourse of the arena, she found what she was looking for. A concession stand had been turned into a bakery. Kira rushed to the counter and purchased a pretzel and a loaf of bread. She stuffed the bread into her bag and quickly began to eat the pretzel. She munched as she wandered farther into the arena concourse.

As she was walking, she saw a sign taped to the wall leading into the actual arena, reading, "Soaps and Laundry," which was on her list of things to acquire. She stepped inside the arena. The sunlight disappeared instantly, but it wasn't dark. Inside, the arena was lit by vendors' candles and lanterns. Each vendor here was perched with their products draped across seats. The air was full of noise. Kira could hear people haggling, laughing and calling out, advertising what they had to sell.

"Clothing repairs! Cheapest you'll find anywhere!"

"Get your seeds here! Seeds!"

"Stay clean, stay healthy! Soaps of all kinds."

Kira's eyes were drawn to what used to be the basketball court floor. There had been a Heat game the night before the Enerjax release, so the wood was still laid out, but now it was fenced in. Inside the fencing was a mass flea market. People were paying, as they exited, for the things they had picked. It all seemed unreal. It was a scene from a video game or science-fiction movie. Kira hadn't really ever been a fan. Now she was living in a sci-fi nightmare.

Kira finished her last bite of pretzel. *Time to get to work.*

She worked her way through the stands, learning quickly to follow the arrows on the floor to avoid going against traffic. After about an hour, she had been able to find all the provisions that they needed for the journey to Europe.

There was only one thing left. Kira had decided to add something special to her list of supplies.

One of the vendors she had bought some crayons from earlier had mentioned that for a price, people could buy special treats. Kira had her mind on a bottle of champagne. She wanted to break it out as a surprise when Joe found Kurt, if he found Kurt. Her heart sank a little bit. She took a deep breath. If Joe believed, so could she. Kira was scared for Joe, scared for how it would crush him if they didn't find Kurt. She hoped not to see that disappointment.

After asking a few shop owners and paying full price for a few unnecessary items, Kira found out about the black market that was taking place downstairs. Under the court's floor was a basement storage room that was now a place for selling things that were rare and less moral. Alcohol of all kinds had become rare in New Miami, so now the only way to get it was by risking a visit downstairs.

Kira rounded a corner in the stairs. A man was leaned against the wall, smoking a joint. The smell of weed smoke was acrid and climbed up her nostrils. He looked at her with bloodshot eyes.

"Hey, baby, you fine. Want to have a little fun?"

Kira just kept walking. She had been catcalled by drunk and high men on a near-nightly basis when she first moved to Miami Beach. She could deal with a little inappropriate behavior. As she walked away, leaving the man in the background, he trailed off, "You don't know what you're missing, girl. Heh, heh, heh."

Kira walked down the dark hallway until she entered the warehouse room. It was a mirror of the market upstairs, a perfect mirror. The layout looked the same, but the atmosphere was the polar opposite. Vendors here were quiet. Money changed hands secretly, and goods were passed in nondescript packages. Other booths backed to side rooms. Men and women would pay the doorman and disappear through the door. Judging from the smell emanating from those rooms, it wasn't a nightclub.

Kira read the doors as she walked by. The first read, "Fight a zombie, make money!" The next read, "OPIUM ROOM." *No subtlety here, I guess*, Kira thought. She continued to walk around until she found a booth with a bottle of champagne drawn on a chalkboard board. The old man stood up on a crutch.

"Hello," Kira greeted him.

"What you want?"

The man was less than hospitable.

"Champagne."

"Why you think I have that? Who told you I have that?"

The man took a very confrontational posture, leaning forward toward Kira.

Kira took a step back but didn't back down. She pointed at the sign.

"Oh, right." The man leaned back. "You got the coin?"

"How much?"

"Ten grams gold."

"I have seven grams silver."

"Then no champagne for you."

Kira had done this a hundred times today. She turned to walk away. The man spoke up. "Wait. Since you're so pretty, I'll give you a bottle for fourteen silver."

"Ten grams silver," Kira replied.

"Twelve grams, and I no tell boss about pretty face."

There was something threatening in his voice.

Kira grabbed a scarf from his table. She wrapped it around her head and face, and handed the man twelve grams. "For the bottle and the scarf."

The old man smiled and reached under his table. He pulled out a box. She opened the top and looked inside. The bottle was there. She closed the box and turned to leave. The old man grabbed her arm. She pulled away.

"Wait," he said. "You hear?"

Kira listened. From the direction of the stairs came a thumping sound. A hush was enveloping the room. It was growing even quieter somehow. Then through the piercing silence, a boisterous laugh echoed.

"I like you. You remind me of niece. Boss coming. You must hide."

"Why?"

"He like pretty girls. Come."

The man handed Kira his crutch. The man then walked to the other side of the stall and directed Kira to where he had been standing behind the booth. It took her a second to get over the fact that the crippled nature of this man was fake.

"Now you one of us. We broken."

Then she realized what he was doing. She must become a crippled shop owner to keep the boss away. She settled into her role. A few seconds later, a large man rounded the corner of the rows.

Kira looked at him in disgust. He had to weigh at least four hundred pounds. A thick sweat dripped from his skin. Drool dripped from his mouth. Each step pounded into the ground, sending shockwaves through his doughy form. He was laughing and drinking straight from a bottle of tequila. He missed part of his mouth with his sip, spilling down his shirtless body. This man was only wearing a massive pair of basketball shorts. He grabbed a handful of something from a nearby stall, ate it in one open-mouthed bite. What Kira saw next stole her breath and heartbeat.

Behind the man, being pulled by a chain leash and wearing leather handcuffs around her wrists, was a young girl about Kira's age. She was crying. Trails of dirt and mud ran down her face. She looked at the ground. The man laughed as he continued down the aisle. He continued to eat and drink all he wanted from the vendors as he passed. The girl tied behind him scuffled along, being yanked from time to time.

After the man and the girl were out of earshot, Kira leaned forward and asked the vendor, "Who the hell was that?"

The man looked surprised and confused at the question. "That boss. You new to here?"

"I gathered that was the boss. Who was the girl?"

"Boss has big hunger."

"I saw that, but what about the girl?

"He have big hunger."

"What about the girl?"

"Him hunger not limited to food and drink."

Kira felt sick.

"Him leader of big gang. So we let him eat and drink what he want."

"And you just let him take girls? What happens to them?"

"If we try and stop the boss, him gang come and kill us."

"What happens to the girls?

"Oh, well once him had him fill, he give them mercy."

"Mercy?"

"Them was his girls, no others can touch again."

"What does mercy mean?"

"He kill.

Kira gasped. "What?"

"You leave. You too good for here. Here meanest and cruelest are king. Other vendors will tell boss men about your pretty face. They come for you next. Leave now."

The man half-pushed Kira from behind the stall and down the aisle. She walked down the row, pulling her head wrap a little tighter, glancing from side to side. Every second felt like excruciating pain. She rounded the corner and saw her freedom. The stairs were in sight, but something held Kira back.

Kira stopped in her tracks. She couldn't leave yet. There was something she needed to do. She turned and headed back into the black market, a purpose set in her mind.

New Miami Mayor's Office:
Outbreak Day +69

A few blocks down from the shopping center, Raul led Joe into the main level of a high-rise. Bodyguards stepped forward, relieving Joe and Raul of weapons. Raul and Joe walked to the elevator. They stepped inside. Raul reached and pressed the penthouse button. The elevator hummed as it climbed the seventy stories to the top. The elevator dinged as the doors opened.

Joe stepped out on marble floors. Sun shined through floor-to-ceiling windows and reflected off crystal chandeliers and golden lamps. A fine Persian rug lay across the floor, and Victorian couches surrounded a glass coffee table. It was a scene from *MTV Cribs*.

"Welcome." A man in his fifties wearing a tailored suit approached from down the hall. His fine shoes clicked with each step. He walked with an ease and a confidence about him. Power and respect seemed to ooze from his tanned skin. "Welcome to my home. I hope your journey here hasn't been too bad."

"You could say it has."

The mayor put his hands in his pockets, and he struck a very serious tone. "I suppose everyone has had a rough couple of months. Did you have trouble in the city?"

"No, Mister Mayor, I made sure he was welcomed like you asked," Raul answered for Joe.

"I asked *him*, Raul."

Raul lowered his head slightly and took a half-step back.

"I have been treated fine here," Joe answered.

"Good. Raul."

"Yes, sir."

"Thank you, you won't be needed here anymore. Why don't you take a bottle from my collection and go home."

"Thank you, sir."

Raul turned and left, stopping only to grab a bottle of whiskey from a box by the elevator. The doors chimed open and shut as he left.

"You're name is Joe, right?

"Yes." Joe looked closer at the man's face. "Do I know you?"

"We've met a couple of times. Follow me." The mayor led Joe to a large office.

The mayor directed Joe to a chair in front of the desk as he took a seat in a large, padded chair himself. He pulled out a picture from the desk drawer and handed it to Joe.

Joe looked at it with shock. The picture was of Joe, the mayor and Stephen Wilkinson. Stephen was a member of Joe's first combat unit. Stephen had been a little eighteen-year-old kid who didn't know what he had signed up for. Joe had watched out for him. Stephen was another young soldier who had reminded Joe of Kurt. It was after their first rotation that Joe had moved to Special Forces. He had never heard from Stephen again. The picture was from when Stephen's parents, Collin and Margerie, had come and visited him. They had been posted at a base, waiting for their next orders. Joe smiled and shook his head. "Mr. Wilkinson, I'm sorry I didn't recognize you. As you can imagine, it's been a hard time."

"Please call me Collin."

"I didn't know you guys lived down here."

"We moved down here last year. We wanted to be closer to Stephen."

"Is he still here?"

"No."

"What happened to him?"

"He . . ." Collin took a deep breath, building up his strength. "He didn't make it. He and his mother were infected right away."

"What?"

"Yeah."

"I'm so sorry."

"It's okay. In a way, I'm glad. I'm glad they didn't see what has become of this place." Collin stood up and looked out the window. "You know, it was you who made Stephen move down here."

"Me?"

"Yeah. He said you told him such great stories about Miami and the beach that he had to come see for himself. I tell you what, I've never seen him so happy. He loved it here. I shudder to think what he would feel about it now."

The mayor was looking out over the city of Miami. From this vantage point, he could see all of what used to be downtown. Skyscrapers stood tall, and glass glinted the sun. It was all a façade, a facelift of death. "Come look at this."

Joe stood and joined Collin at the window.

"See that ring of downed buildings?

"Yeah. I noticed that earlier."

"That was my idea. In my youth, I was a volunteer firefighter. So many times, it seemed like a blaze was unstoppable. All we could do was retreat and burn down a line through the forest. The only risk then was embers flying in the wind. Here, there were no embers to catch flight. It allowed those of us left to fight controlled numbers. We survived."

"That's all we can do now."

"No, it's not. Let me show you something."

Joe followed Collin as he went to the elevator. Collin stepped inside and pressed the lobby button.

"Where are we going?" Joe asked.

"The building next door is used for special projects. There is something you need to see."

The ride to the bottom was silent. After the doors opened, Collin had the bodyguards give Joe his weapons back and then led the way to a side door. A small alley separated the buildings. They quickly crossed over and entered the next building. It was an office structure for medical testing. Joe passed room after room of medical equipment sitting idly in the dark. Up ahead, lights shined brightly. The interior labs were still operational. Inside, members were filling vials with some liquid. Collin stopped in front of the window. He was watching with pride.

"When the outbreak started, everyone was just trying to survive." Collin hung his head and shook it. "We are all still just trying to survive. It won't last. We are outnumbered, and the undead don't tire or hunger or thirst. Humans are lower on the food chain than they are. Evolution dictates our demise."

"That's kind of a depressing way of looking at it," Joe said.

"Well it's the truth. We are all going to die. Well, unless we do something about it."

Joe looked at the people filling vial after vial. "Did you find a cure?

"No, I wish, but we didn't. That's not to say we didn't try. In front of you are all the remaining doctors and medical researchers we could find. Even with their combined knowledge, there was no way to reverse the reaction. We did make a breakthrough though."

"Really?"

"Yeah, you see, one of the doctors, one night, after failing to find the cure, got really drunk. He started wandering through the floors of the building upstairs. Well we had cleared the building already, so we knew there was no zombie life anywhere. What we didn't know is that the armed men had come across something. To them, it was just a room of slaughter, but to the scientist, it was a fundamental change in his thinking. Three floors above us is a large room. It had been the cafeteria in a previous life. In that room is a pile of dead bodies. Nearly twenty people had gotten cornered in there. Well the zombies found them. Actually two zombies found them. It was a blood bath. Those two zombies killed and ate almost every part of those people, and I don't mean munched on them or ate a finger. I mean, whole bodies, gone. All we could find were little scraps of people and name tags that had been ripped off. Those small pieces of scrap were all that was left. It was a pure feast. Can you guess what happened to those two zombies next?"

"They kept searching for more food?" Joe said.

"They died," Collin responded. "Actually died! Never to rise again."

"What?"

"I know, right? That's exactly how that scientist felt! Yet in that moment, he understood something. That's when this scientist realized he had been trying something impossible. We had been trying to reclaim the past. We had been hoping to cure everyone and go back to the way things were. That's not possible. What he needed to focus on was replicating what happened to those two zombies. We need to kill them all. We just need an efficient way."

"We already know how to kill them. Headshots."

"No, we need something easier. That scientist, there in that room, looking at blood smears and two rather fat, bloated, dead zombie bodies, had an epiphany. They had literally eaten themselves to death. Their gluttonous hunger was the key to killing them. So he came back to the lab, after sobering up some, and did something amazing. He found a way to kill zombies quickly and easily. With the liquid in there that they are putting into those tubes, we can kill the creatures in droves.

"Is that a nerve gas or something?"

"Something like that. It's actually concentrated Enerjax enhancer."

"Enerjax? That's what started this whole thing!"

"Yes! It's also what can end it. The Enerjax turns up your caloric burn. The intent was less laziness. What they didn't expect was that the resultant increase in body temperature literally cooks the brain, turning you into a zombie."

"How does that explain raising things from the dead or keeping those creatures alive?"

"All it takes is one dormant cell. The energy produced can replicate quickly. As for giving them more than normal life traits, they don't need a heart or lungs. Our body uses blood and the heart to deliver oxygen to our cells, allowing us to function. Their bodies actually use pure cellular energy to function."

"So that chemical in there does what to kill them?"

"It sends the effects of Enerjax into overdrive. That's what happened to the zombies upstairs. They ate so much that their bodies went into crazy overdrive and burnt themselves out. Imagine a fire. If you added gas to it little by little, it could keep burning for as long as there was fuel to consume. But if you threw a ton of gas in all at once, a massive explosion would consume all the fuel at once, also snuffing out the fire. Fighting fire with fire."

"But you just said that we could wait until they run out of fuel. So outlasting them is an option too?"

"Hypothetically, yes, but we don't know how long that takes. We have a zombie chained up in a room down the hall that has been starving all winter and hasn't died yet. This way, we can kill the plague now."

"Here, let me show you what I mean." Collin led Joe down a dimly lit hall and opened a door. Light flooded out the second he cracked the door open. He paused before opening it fully. "We keep this room well lit for observation purposes, although looking at these things is not exactly a pleasant experience in full light. Just warning you." The mayor stepped in. Joe followed him.

Instantly Joe's heart dropped. Chained to a wall by its wrists and ankles was a large zombie wearing a Hawaiian shirt. He was softly thrashing, trying to escape his tight bonds, trying to feed on the new entrants. Joe couldn't believe his eyes. Even with the sunken eye sockets, bleeding nose and drool dripping from its veined lips, the zombie was instantly recognizable. It was, or rather used to be, Aaron.

While Joe was caught in a zone, staring at the deformed version of someone he had helped rescue just a few months ago, the mayor had moved to a table that sat against the far wall. He picked up a clipboard and said, "Fifty-three days."

"What?" Joe asked.

"It's been fifty-three days since we captured this one. At least fifty-three days since it last ate."

"It has a name!"

"I'm sure he did at some point, but who cares now? Odds are, anyone who cared about him and anyone he cared about are gone now. So here *it* hangs, starving but never dying."

"You can't just let him hang here like this."

"I'm not going to." The mayor picked up a handheld tranquilizer gun that sat on the table next to the clipboard and aimed it at Aaron. The mayor shot a

NEW WORLD **207**

dart filled with the Enerjax booster into Aaron's stomach.

"Wait!" Joe yelled too late. The zombie that Aaron had become quickly grew angrier, shaking violently. Seizures overtook its form as foam oozed from its mouth. Then in an instant, in a blink of the eye, it stopped.

"Simple as that. It's over," Collin said, shrugging his shoulders.

Joe had been clenching his fist. He let it relax. *At least it's over now for him.*

"So you see, this can end the zombie plague rather fast. We are starting production, and soon we can start cleansing this earth. Hopefully start over and make the world better. With this solution, we can fly over cities and crop dust with this stuff. Soldiers can use the darts or handheld gas bombs. We could use a fire hose and spray zombie crowds with it. Hell, everyday people could spray it with Super Soakers. It absorbs through the skin, so everything is possible."

"Wouldn't you just be polluting the world and the water?"

"No. We have developed a modified Enerjax enhancer. This one only bonds with Enerjax, and it renders itself inactive after twenty-four hours."

"So there isn't a risk?"

"Not unless you're already infected."

"So why aren't you already using it?"

"It's complicated. Until this week, we didn't have the supplies for mass production. We rely on consistent shipments from convoys returning from

Europe. Before I can secure enough of the supplies we need, we have to provide this chemical as a shipment to the leader of Newlantis. Some of the materials are hard to come by these days. He has a stockpile, but we have to prove it works first before he'll start a new trade of chemical zombie kill, to get the supplies we need to make it."

"What does this have to do with me?"

"You came to New Miami to join a convoy, right?"

"That's right."

"Well we have one leaving, tomorrow morning. In most cases, we require you to stay a full convoy cycle here in town before joining. We want to make sure not to send a pirate into their midst."

"I can't wait that long."

"And I need someone to help me. I need you to do something for me.

"Which is?"

"I need you to carry the shipment of the drug with you to Europe."

"Me? Why don't you send one of your men on the trip?"

"Two reasons. One, I can't spare the men here. A gang is constantly fighting us and really is on the brink of overthrowing our small semblance of a government here. I need all the men I have. Two, if I sent one of my men, he would be ambushed before he reached the docks. They are well known by the people."

Joe thought about it.

Collin continued. "Look, Joe, I trust you. I know the kind of man you are. Stephen told me a lot about all the times you helped him. You coming here has solved a major problem I have had. I need you to do this."

"I'll need you to help arrange one other thing," Joe said.

"What's that?"

Joe leaned in, whispering into Collin's ear. They were alone, but he wanted to ensure no one else heard this request.

Collin smiled. "I'll do my best."

"Okay then."

"Great! Come back to the tower tonight after dark, and retrieve the drug. I'll be packing several vials in a silver briefcase. You come pick it up, get back to the boat, head out to the convoy, get out of New Miami and be on your way."

New Miami Market: Outbreak Day +69

Kira skulked down the row of vendor booths. After a short walk, she saw what she had come for. The young girl she had watched being pulled by the massive, horrid man known as the boss was sitting on the ground. Her leash had been tethered to a handle mounted on the wall, next to a door. On the door, a board read, "Zombie Fight Club." Kira could hear muffled cheers from inside. She watched as a man walked past the girl, looking at her for a moment. Then seeming to notice something, he stepped back from her and went inside the fight-club door. Cheers, screams and laughs emanated out of it as it opened.

Kira looked around. No one was watching the young girl. No one was around. Judging by the man's reaction, Kira assumed that everyone must know this is the boss's girl. No one would dare cross him, no one but Kira. Kira studied the girl.

She was kneeling, her hands tied together in a way that made her look like a Disney princess wishing on a nonexistent star. Tear streaks marked her face. Kira could see red rash areas around her leather handcuffs. The chain that was used as a leash was looped through the handle on the wall and locked with a thick master lock. A smaller yet sturdy lock held her leather handcuffs shut.

Kira moved quickly and quietly to the girl. The girl pulled away from Kira in fear. Kira tried to calm her, but the girl continued to slide away from her. Kira pulled off the head wrap, showing her face to the girl. The girl calmed instantly.

Kira pulled out the combat knife Joe had given her. The girl pulled away again. Kira put her finger to her lips, signaling quiet. She then slowly reached and grabbed the leather cuffs. She cut the girl free after a little sawing with the knife. The girl pulled free of the bindings and rubbed her wrists. Kira wrapped the scarf around the girl's face and led her by the hand down the aisle of vendors.

When they reached the stairs, they leaped upward, skipping steps. After reaching the top, in less than a minute, they were in the light now. It was refreshing, the sunlight a stark difference to the dark underworld they had just left. They paused for a moment, catching their breath after their hasty escape.

The girl took off the scarf and said, "Thank you."

"Are you okay?" Kira asked, looking at the girl's red wrists.

"Yes, they're just friction burns. Thank you. He just took me this morning. If you hadn't helped, I don't want to know what would have happened to me."

"What's your name?"

"I'm Jolie."

"Nice to meet you. I'm Kira."

"Why did you help me?"

"What?"

"Why would you risk your life for me?"

"Because you needed help." Kira was confused by the question.

"Sorry, I'm just not used to people helping each other. Around here, it's every man for himself."

"Well I'm not that way. Neither is the man I'm traveling with."

"Must be nice."

"It is. So where is your family?"

"Dead."

"I'm sorry. Zombies?"

"No. The boss sent his men after me. Well my brother and father tried to fight them off. The boss killed them both in front of me. He called it a wedding gift."

Kira's face showed how appalled she was.

"Speaking of which," Jolie continued as she handed the scarf back to Kira, "you need to hide. The boss is going to come for you. No one crosses him and gets away with it."

"What about you?" Kira asked.

"I'll have to run. I don't know where, but I don't have any other options."

"Why don't you come with us?"

"What?"

"We're leaving for Europe. You could join us."

"Are you serious? You don't even know me."

"So?"

"Well you don't know the kind of person I am. I could murder you all."

"Are you going to?"

"Well no."

"Good, then you can come with us. Look, I saw you tied up down there. You weren't dreaming of revenge or hate. You were wishing to be saved. You still have goodness inside you. I can see it. We have an awesome boat. It's a Marquis 630 docked at the temporary mooring. There is room for you, and we can all get away. The man I'm with is meeting with the mayor right now, and then we are leaving ASAP."

"I don't know."

"I'm serious. The boat is called *La Vida Dulce*. You can leave this shitty place and live the sweet life with us. But there is one thing."

"What's that?" Jolie asked, suspicious of the good fortune that was coming her way.

"You have to be okay with kids. Innocent, sweet kids."

Jolie teared up. "I didn't know there was any innocence left in the world."

"Come on. Let's go," Kira said.

"Okay."

Kira and Jolie quickly walked past the vendors, heading for the marina.

Just around the corner of the stairs stood a man, puffing on his joint. He had watched two girls sprint from the underbelly of the market. They hadn't seen him sitting by the wall at the bottom of the stairs as they bolted by. He knew they were up to no good, so he followed them.

The conversation he had just listened to was more than he had expected or could have hoped for. He smiled as he walked toward the "Zombie Fight Club" door. The boss would be grateful for this information.

New Miami Harbor: Outbreak Day +69

Joe walked down the steps leading to the boat docks in the marina. One of Raul's men walked close to him, an AK-47 slung over his shoulder. Joe nodded to the man. The man nodded back. After a few minutes of walking down floating docks, he was home. He walked up the stairs of the boat and knocked on the door.

Knock-knock-knock . . .

Knock . . .

Knock-knock-knock-knock.

Kira opened it and hugged him hello. Joe looked behind her and saw a face from the past. He released Kira, staring at their new traveling companion.

"Jolie?"

"Joe?"

Joe stood in shock, staring and frozen for a half-second. The next second, he was running across the living room of the yacht, picking Jolie up in a big, embracing hug. Jolie laughed and cried as she hugged Joe back.

Kira felt a tinge of anxiety color her yellow. She and Joe had shared a wonderful night, but she couldn't compete with history. If Joe and this girl were something before the zombie apocalypse, then she could be a way for him to reclaim the past. Kira could never offer him that.

Joe released the girl and held her by her shoulders. They were both crying at this point. He looked her in the eyes. "I can't believe you're alive. How?" he asked.

"Well Danny, Dad and I survived the initial outbreak." Jolie's face drained of color, and her tears changed from joy to anger. In the past day of captivity, she had cried out all her despair. "Then that fat piece of shit came to take me. They tried to hold him off, so he killed them. He would have done worse to me if Kira hadn't cut me loose."

"What?" Joe glanced back and forth at Kira and Jolie.

Jolie told the story as best she could, not sparing any obscenities when it came to describing the boss. Jolie turned to Kira. "Yeah. So she saved me, saved me from what the boss was calling a wedding-night celebration to come." She shuddered as she said those words.

Joe turned to Kira. "You did that?"

She quietly nodded.

Joe leaned in and gave her a deep kiss. She hadn't expected it. After a second, she melted into his lips. He released the kiss and hugged her. He whispered in her ear, "Thank you."

He let her go and sat down on the couch, letting his weight fall and exhaling in relaxation. "What a day."

Kira asked, "So I guess you guys know each other?"

Joe laughed. "You could say that."

Jolie understood what Joe didn't. Kira expected that their relationship was more than friendship. "We have been friends since we were little. Well Danny, my brother, and Joe went to school with each other from kindergarten through high school. Kurt, his brother, and I are the same age too, so our families became super close. We used to go on family vacations together and everything. The four of us—Danny, Joe, Kurt and I—were known as the four amigos. They were like extra brothers to me. Danny and Joe even . . . whoa. When Danny got sick, do you remember your promise?"

"Promise?" Kira asked.

Joe answered. "A couple years ago, I was going overseas, and Danny had lymphoma. We were both so afraid, and so were Kurt and Jolie. They were afraid to lose their older brothers. We . . . we were each afraid of leaving a younger sibling behind unprotected. For us, taking care of our little brother and sister was a major concern. Well we promised each other and them," Joe pointed at Jolie, "that no matter what, if anything happened to one of us, the other would be there as an older brother. I think we made the promise more for each other than anything. It gave Danny a reason to fight and me a reason to keep fighting. Well we both made it."

"But now you're honoring that promise." Kira had a tear running down her cheek.

"Yes he is, and Danny is looking down somewhere, smiling," Jolie added.

"I didn't save you. She did." Joe was pointing at Kira.

"Yes, but you saved me first. So in a roundabout way, you still saved her," Kira said.

"You both saved me. Thank you so much. Earlier today when I was sitting in that place, do you know what I was doing? I was praying for God to kill me."

Joe and Kira both swallowed hard.

Jolie continued. "I had no reason to live any longer. I had no will to go on. Now I have family again."

Joe smiled. "More than you know."

"What do you mean?"

"Kira, have you introduced her to the others?"

"Not yet, we just got back to the boat ourselves. Christine answered and recognized that I had a stranger with me. So they went downstairs and hid."

"Smart kids," Joe said.

"That's right, the kids," Jolie said, looking back and forth between Joe and Kira.

"Not ours, well not in that way at least," Kira answered.

Joe stood up. "Jolie, you're a big sister now."

Joe walked to the stairs heading down to the bedrooms. "Jack, Christine, Elizabeth, it's okay. You can come up." The three kids peeked their heads around the corner in single file. Two of them hung onto his legs, hiding behind him, shying away from the new person in their home. Jack was in Joe's arms, staring at her. "Guys, I want you to meet Jolie. She is a good friend of mine from when I was younger, when I was your age, Jack. She's very nice."

Jack hadn't broken his stare. "Where is she going to sleep?"

Joe hadn't thought about that, but it made sense to give her the bed the three children had been sharing. It was more of an adult's room. "Well that's the good surprise I have for you all." He had to word it correctly so that it didn't seem like Jolie was taking something away from them. "You know how we have talked about building a fort in your playroom?" Jack bobbed his head in fast, excited nods. "Well we are going to, and you all get to stay there with all your toys. How does that sound?"

Jack nodded again enthusiastically. The two girls nodded as well, still clinging to Joe's pant legs.

Jolie got down in a crouch. She brushed her hair back from her face. "Hello there, I'm Jolie. It's very nice to meet you. What's your name?" She was looking at Christine.

"Christine. What happened to your wrists?" Christine asked.

"Oh this, it's nothing. It's nice to meet you, Christine." She turned her attention to Elizabeth. "What's your name?" Elizabeth didn't answer but hid farther behind Joe's leg.

Jack answered for her. "Her name is Elizabeth, and I'm Jack. Do you like toys?"

Jolie stood up, looking at Jack. "Actually I love toys. Do you have some cool ones?"

Jack's eyes lit up. He squirmed, and Joe put him down. "Come on, I'll show you." He extended his little hand, and she took it. He led her down the stairs. Christine and Elizabeth followed, wanting to be part of the show.

Joe and Kira were alone on the main deck now.

He hugged her tightly. "Thank you so much for doing this. You have no idea how much this means to me."

"Then you're not upset at all?"

"Upset? Why would I be upset?"

"Because I did what you told me not to do. I broke the normal way of things."

"No, I'm not mad. You saved someone close to me."

Kira leaned closer Joe.

Joe eventually pushed away. "I have to go back out tonight."

"What? Why?"

"The mayor has given us a spot on the convoy, but I have be a courier for something for him."

"What do you have to carry?"

Joe told Kira the whole story, only interrupted occasionally by laughter echoing up from downstairs. After he was finished telling his tale, Kira wiped a tear from her face. "Poor Aaron."

"Yeah," Joe said.

"Well do you have time for a family dinner before going back?" Kira asked.

"Yeah, that I can do," Joe said.

Kira began cooking a late dinner as Joe and Jolie helped the kids set up the fort in the playroom. The energetic burst had tired the kids out. Shortly after dinner, the little ones were ready for bedtime. Kira went to read then a book and tuck them in. Joe stayed upstairs to get his gear ready. Jolie had just finished a shower erasing the day's events. She came and sat by Joe as he reassembled his M4 assault rifle.

"Hey, how was your shower?" Joe asked Jolie.

"Great! I feel like a whole new person," Jolie replied.

"That's good."

"Hey, Joe, I didn't ask earlier, but Kira mentioned we're leaving for Europe in the morning."

"That's not really a question."

"Well why?"

"You want to stay here?" Joe asked sarcastically.

"No obviously, but there are uninfected islands in the Caribbean that we could be going to, and the trip isn't as dangerous."

"Kurt. We need to go get him."

"What?" Jolie asked with shock in her voice.

"Kurt is in Russia. He's alive."

"Oh wait, he was on semester abroad, that's right. Wow. He's alive?"

"Yeah."

"You've actually talked to him?"

"I missed the call, but he left me a message." Joe looked at Jolie, making eye contact. "314."

Jolie nodded. "What time do we leave?"

"The convoy leaves at 9:00 a.m."

"Okay."

Jolie stood up and started to walk downstairs. Joe looked up from the gun he was working on. He had been a little cold. He was starting to get into a focused zone. "Jolie."

She stopped and turned. Joe sat with an open mouth, unable to find the words. She understood. "I know, do what you have to do."

Joe finished his gun work and put on the rest of his gear, including the head wrap the girls had brought home. It was from the black market, giving instant credibility to his image of intimidation. Someone who had that rag must be someone unafraid of the drug dens.

Joe left the yacht and headed toward the lab facility.

New Miami Mayor's Office: Outbreak Day +69

Joe unwrapped his face before approaching the mayor's building. The men took him inside, where Collin was waiting with the case.

"Thank you for doing this. This may be one of the most important missions in the future of mankind."

"It gets me to my brother. That's what I care about."

"Joe, I know I won't see you again, so I'd like to tell you while I have the chance. Thank you. Thank you for being such an example to my son. The life he had after he met you was full of happiness and goal setting. He was a different person after he got to know you. Thank you for that. I hope you find Kurt and somewhere you can call home, somewhere far away from here."

Joe shook his hand, took the case and fixed the wrap around his face once again. He headed out for the harbor. Soon he would be sleeping in the arms of a woman he loved and then waking up and leaving to find his brother.

New Miami Harbor: Outbreak Day +69

Joe walked down the stairs heading into the marina. This time, Raul's man was nowhere to be found. *Must be slacking*, Joe thought.

Joe was about thirty feet away from *La Vida Dulce* when he noticed something wasn't right. The back door was wide open. The interior lights were shining out against the black night. Joe stopped. He bent down, grabbed a rope that was tied to a mooring point and tied the case around it. He pushed the case under the floating dock and put his rifle to his shoulder. Moving slowly, Joe climbed the stairs of *La Vida Dulce* and assessed the situation. It was dead quiet. Then he heard a slurp. He moved in quickly, jerking his rifle to the figure sitting on the couch, sipping a glass of water. His head filled Joe's sights. A waif of a man sat wearing a well-worn black suit. His face was gaunt and showed a five-o'clock shadow. This man looked at Joe in an upsettingly relaxed manner.

"Put the gun down."

"Who the fuck are you?" Joe spat out at him.

"Put the gun down," the man said, unfazed.

"Who are you?"

The man set the glass of water on the table in front of him. "If you want to see either of the girls again, put the gun down." He was still a strange, confident calm.

The man had an honest threat to his words.

Joe lowered his sights from the man but did not let go of the rifle. "Who are you?"

"I'm Jones. I'm the voice of your new leader, or soon-to-be leader at least."

Joe risked a glance toward the stairs.

The man understood his thoughts. "I'm not an animal. The kids are asleep and will be untouched."

"Where are the girls?"

"Oh, they're safe for now, but only if you do exactly as you're told."

"What do you want?"

"The boss has noticed that you can meet with the mayor anytime you wish, even with weapons. That's never happened. Well the boss thinks you might be able to do something for him, something that would settle your debt."

"Debt? I don't owe him anything."

"Oh, but you do. You see, your companion stole something from him. Being that she is yours to watch here, you are responsible for her actions."

"How much?"

"I'm sorry."

"How much to pay back the boss for Jolie to reimburse him?"

"It's not that simple anymore."

"Why not?"

"The boss has lost face because of your girl's actions. Do you know what that means around here? Your reputation is everything. Now the only way to reclaim what his reputation has lost is to do something big. That's where you come in. Your soon-to-be leader, the man you may have heard of as 'the boss,' wants what the mayor is hiding in that secret facility of his."

Joe knew from his training that telling a straightforward lie was easy to detect, but if you mix a sliver of the truth in with your lie, it can confound even the best lie detector. "I know what it is. He showed me."

"Really?"

"Yeah."

"What is it?"

"No."

"No?"

"I'm not going to tell you that or where is it.

"We know where the building is."

"But you don't know where in the building it is, and you'll get caught with your pants down if you send men to find it. The mayor told me about the delicate balance your groups have."

"Okay, so you will bring it to us. You bring us his secret weapon and you get to leave with your girls intact."

"How do I know I can trust the boss?"

"You don't, and I wouldn't, but you don't have a choice."

The man led Joe outside on the back deck. He closed the door behind him and locked it. He handed the key to Joe with a crooked smile.

Joe turned to leave the yacht.

"Oh, and G.I. Joe, hurry before the boss gets hungry for breakfast. He loves to have dessert with his meals."

Joe hurried out the door, heading for the mayor's building at a double-time march. All he could think about were Kira and Jolie.

What the hell happened? Why did Kira open the door for anyone but him?

La Vida Dulce, a Few Hours Earlier: Outbreak Day +69

Kira came upstairs, joining Jolie.

"Are they sleeping?" Jolie asked.

"Yeah," Kira answered. "They liked the idea of having a sleepover in their playroom, so you have a bedroom to yourself."

"Thanks. Thanks again for everything. I can't believe how much of a whirlwind this day has been."

"Yeah, seriously. This morning we were in Key West. It's amazing what can happen in a day. Did Joe leave already?"

"Yeah, he just did."

Kira felt a tinge of sadness and disappointment that Joe had not said goodbye to her. He had never left without doing so. Maybe his head was so focused on the mission at hand that it had just slipped his train of thought. Still, she felt cheated.

A knock came at the door.

"Oh, he must have forgotten something," Jolie said as she got up and unlocked the door.

Kira yelled, "Wait!"

It was too late. Jolie was already sliding the door open. On the other side stood a skinny man in a suit, and behind him on the back-deck couch sat the boss surrounded by three other men with guns. Jolie let out a small shriek, seeing the men. She covered her mouth with her hands as she took a step backward.

The boss laughed a guttural bellow. His fat rolls squeezing out the side of his pants jiggled. The skinny man in the oily black suit who had knocked on the door leaned forward, showing a set of jagged teeth in an evil smile. "Good evening, ladies."

New Miami Mayor's Office: Outbreak Day +69

Joe walked up to the stairs of the mayor's building. The bodyguards escorted him inside, where he stood waiting in the lobby. Every second felt like an hour. The elevator chimed, and Collin walked out of the elevator.

Before Joe had a chance to say anything, Collin asked, "What happened?"

"It's safe, but we have a problem. Some man named 'the boss' has kidnapped the girl I have been traveling with and a friend I've had for a lifetime." Joe was angry. "I need to get them back."

"I told you I can't go to war with him."

"You're going to. I have an idea, one that is going to solve this for you forever."

"What's the plan?"

"Well it goes like this."

New Miami Market: Outbreak Day +69

Joe squeezed the handle of the case and released it. He could feel the sweat building in his palms. Everything needed to go as planned or none of them were getting out of this alive. He breathed deeply and wiped a bead of sweat from his forehead. There was no need to hide his nerves. He was walking into a gang lord's den, most likely to his doom. Not being nervous would be a sure tell that something was going on, so Joe let his nerves show.

He walked down the ramp leading toward the loading-dock area for the arena. The entire area was lit by one powerful flood light. It turned everything a ghostly orange hue against the dark night.

When he was ten feet from the service garage door, four men opened it and filed out. Three of them pointed rifles at Joe. The fourth was the skinny man in the silky black suit from earlier, named Jones.

Jones spoke to Joe. "Welcome, I see your trip to the mayor has been fruitful," he said while pointing at the case.

"I got what you want. Where are the girls?"

"You will get your friends back once you've delivered the case."

"I'm delivering it. Bring the girls out now."

Jones let out a cynical laugh. "Oh, you aren't delivering it to me. You have to take it to the boss. He has your girls. Inside."

Joe took a step toward the group of men. They all aimed their weapons a little more tightly toward Joe's face. He stopped, holding up the hand not carrying the case, showing his palm, trying to calm them down.

Jones spoke again. "We aren't as trusting as the mayor here. You will need to leave your guns outside. That trash can there, put your guns in the dumpster. All of them."

Joe slid the rifle off his shoulder and walked to the dumpster. He used the butt of the gun to push the lid open and let the rifle slide inside. Joe turned and didn't even get a chance to take a step.

"Stop!" Jones commanded. "I said all your weapons!"

Joe reached behind his back and pulled his pistol out of the rear holster. He put that inside dumpster as well. "Happy?"

"And the other weapon."

Joe looked at Jones. Joe decided to gamble, to call this man's bluff. There was no way Jones could see the knife hidden down his pants, holstered tightly to his inner thigh. "I don't have any other guns. That's all I carry."

Jones stared at Joe.

Jones waved one of the men over. The man patted Joe down. However, the thug didn't feel high enough on his inner thigh to feel the knife.

Always have a weapon, Joe thought. *Maybe there is a chance this will work out.*

The man finished his pat-down of Joe and nodded to Jones. "Follow me," Jones said.

Joe walked past the man who had just patted him down. As Joe stepped inside the garage door, the man, who was trailing behind him, pushed him forward. There were two men standing next to Jones already inside. Another two stood on each side of the garage door. They pulled chains, lowering the door behind Joe. One last man in the room was leaning on a pillar just a few feet to Joe's left. Joe continued to scan the room.

It was an open loading dock. A small entry door was next to the garage door the men were still working on lowering. A metal folding chair was positioned next to the door. *Must be a guard post*, Joe thought. Joe next focused on a pair of generators that were running a power supply to the security office, two overhead flood lights and a service elevator, its doors standing open to the right of the bay. There was another man inside watching camera feeds, which Joe had missed on his first glance. The garage door finished closing with a loud bang. "Let's go," Jones said.

Joe looked back at the entry door. One of the men who had been pulling on the chains to close the garage sat down in the chair. The other walked past Joe, heading for the security office. Joe was once again prodded to move forward.

The small group stepped into the elevator: Jones, Joe and two men. A third man, the one who had been trailing the group and giving Joe motivation to move forward, pulled a key out of his pocket. He inserted it in the club-level button and turned it, and the button lit up. The man then stepped back out of the elevator. The doors closed, and a soft hum could be heard as the elevator began to ascend. Joe stood on one side of the elevator lobby, holding his case tight, expecting the men to turn on him at any moment. He had oriented himself so his back was toward a wall. The others all stood on the opposite side, watching Joe intently. The ride up was painfully slow. The elevator was meant for cargo, not quickness. While waiting for the elevator to reach the luxury floors, Joe ran the plan over again in his mind. Inside the case were twenty syringes. Sixteen of them contained Enerjax, and four contained a simple IV solution dyed the same color. The safe needles were the one on the far left, the two in the middle and the second from the right. Joe had to make sure he remembered that fact. If the boss wanted to test the liquid, Joe had built in a plan to trick him.

The elevator reached the luxury floor with a ding. The doors opened at suite level. Two men with guns were waiting as the doors opened. Jones confidently strode past the men. "This way," he said. The two men with guns, who rode up with Joe, walked behind Joe as they made their way down the ornate hallway. After about a minute, the group all reached a double-doored room. Joe recognized the name placard. This was previously the owner's box.

Jones pushed both doors open, making a grand, announced entrance. Joe followed closely behind. As

Joe entered the room, the pall of cigar smoke and the smell of drug use almost made him gag.

He scanned the room from left to right. The box was huge, expansive and richly decorated. This was a true suite. There was a kitchenette to the left. A man standing there squinted at Joe as he rested against the countertop. Straight across the room from the double doors were rows of seats, facing the arena. It was hard to see how many seats there were because of a mass of solid obstruction. Against the back of the seats was positioned a love seat that served as a large chair for the man known as 'the boss.' This giant, grotesque human sat watching Joe. Jones had walked to the boss's right-hand side. Joe spotted two other men in the room, ahead of him. One massive, strong man stood on the other side of the boss. He was easily six five and looked to be three hundred pounds of pure muscle. The other man stood off to Joe's right.

"Joe!" a voice shouted.

As Joe had shifted his glances to the right to get a better look at that man, Kira and Jolie had recognized his face. They were sitting on a small couch, with that man standing over them, watching the two prisoners. Kira tried to stand at the sight of Joe, but the man pushed her back down.

A flushing noise sounded, and another man stepped out of a bathroom. He took a place next to the girls, joining the other watchman.

The two men following Joe closed the doors behind him, one giving Joe a forceful shove, urging him forward.

Joe walked forward. Soon he was standing just feet in front of the fattest man he had ever seen. His fat wiggled with each breath the man took. Skin lesions lined his elbows and knees. Blue bruises and swollen blood vessels spidered everywhere along his folds. Slobber dripped down his chin as he held a cigar between his lips. An oily sheen covered the half-naked man. Only a pair of basketball shorts, stretched to their limit, covered his privates. While the shorts spared the eyes, the nose was not so lucky. This man smelled like rotting flesh. Joe imagined that under the rolls and folds were spots on his body that hadn't been washed in some time.

"Welcome, Jossseph, welcome to myyy home." The man's drunken slur added more disgust to his appearance. "Do yooou have what I askked you for?"

"Yes. I have the immunization," Joe answered.

The answer clearly upset the boss. Jones, who had moved to the boss's right side and was eyeing a neglected bottle of beer, reacted similarly. "Immunization?" he asked with a slight mixture of anger and fear.

"Yeah, the mayor's secret. His immunization to the zombie plague. It's why his men never turn."

The boss reached out and grabbed Jones's suit coat, pulling him close. The body-odor stench emanating from the boss made Jones pull his nose away.

"You said it was a weapon!" the boss said, the last syllable spat at Jones.

"But . . . but, boss, this is better."

"Hoow?" he yelled at the man in his grasp.

"Uh, uh," Jones stammered. He was trying to think fast but was failing.

Joe spoke up, helping Jones, but helping his own cause more. "Sir. If you will allow me to speak."

The boss looked at him, still holding Jones. "Well? Whhhat?"

"You can use this. Use it as a way to get the people on your side. The mayor has been hoarding this cure, keeping it away. You can be a savior to the people. The man of the people who helped the poor. You're the man who saved the ones who are really in danger if a zombie makes it through the blockades, not some elitist."

The boss let go of Jones, leaning forward on the love seat, placing his hand on his chin, thinking.

Joe continued. "All you have to do is give a few of the twenty needles I have in this case to some of the citizens, for free."

"Ffffor free?" the boss spat out in an angry confusion.

Joe held his hand up, palm out. "Only a couple, not the whole case. Just a few leftover after immunizing yourself and your men. Then you tell the people that the vials you gave away were the only ones you could get your hands on, but if they help you and join your gang, you can overthrow the mayor and will be able to make more. It's at his medical clinic next to the tower. Once you're mayor, you can reward those who are loyal and helped you. Or set the price for the cure and have ultimate power." Joe finished the last part of his sales pitch by clenching his fist.

"See, boss," Jones jumped in, attempting to capitalize on the moment. "Yes, we can use this to our advantage."

"Our advantage?" Joe asked in an accusatory tone. "Don't you mean his advantage?" Joe pointed at the boss and looked at him. "You are the boss, right?"

"What the fuck did you just ssssay?" the boss nearly yelled back at Joe, clearly insulted.

Joe committed more to his play, maintaining an innocent curiosity in his voice. "Sorry. I didn't mean any disrespect. The way he said 'our advantage' just made it feel like you two were a team."

"We are a team," Jones said.

The boss cocked his head in Jones's direction, anger in his eyes.

Jones quickly backtracked. "I mean that we're a team like Batman and Robin. You give me commands, and I do everything for you."

"Are . . . are . . . are . . . are you calling meee lazy?" the boss asked, even angrier.

"No! What? No, I didn't mean it like that," Jones said, fear filling his voice.

"Then whaat did you meeeeean?"

"I just meant that . . . I'm loyal to you. I've done everything for you."

"You've done everrrrything for meeee?" Everything Jones said seemed to make the boss even more pissed off.

"Boss! Stop! Calm down. Let's just take these needles, kill this man and—"

Joe spoke up, interrupting Jones. "You're giving him commands now?"

"You shut the fuck up!" Jones snapped at Joe.

"I'm just saying that sounded like a command," Joe said.

"You shut your mouth! Someone kill him!" Jones screamed at the room.

"Now he's commanding your men," Joe said, directing his message to the boss.

"Kill him!" Jones screamed again, this time darting his attention between men in the room. The men didn't move, unsure of what to do. "What is wrong with you? I'm telling you to kill that man. Obey my orders!"

"No!" the boss yelled. "That's enough of you making orders in my room."

"What?" Jones asked, surprised and insulted. "You really aren't going to kill him? You're taking this fucker's side on this?"

"Now he's questioning you, in front of your men," Joe said, doing everything he could to escalate the situation. "Not only did he lie to you about a weapon, but he's also blatantly disrespecting you in front of subordinates."

"That's enough from you!" Jones pulled a gun out of his suit coat and stepped toward Joe. "If they won't do it, I'll do it myself." He started to raise it toward Joe. Jones's arm aim had reached about thigh high when his chest exploded. Joe was spattered with blood. Jones dropped to the floor. Behind him, the boss was standing, a shotgun pistol Joe recognized as "The Judge" in his hand. The boss held the pistol steady, suddenly appearing sober. "Show me the needles. Now."

Joe quickly opened the case, holding it in the air in front of his body, shielding himself as well as displaying the twenty syringes neatly secured in the case.

"You have seen them injected?" the boss asked Joe, still pointing the gun at him.

"Yes I have, sir," Joe said.

"Inject yourself with one," the boss commanded.

Joe paused for a moment, feeling out the situation and deciding to stick with his plan. It was working up to this point, and he was prepared for this. "But, sir, the mayor already gave me an injection and then proved it worked by forcing me to be bitten." Joe pulled up his shirt sleeve, showing a scabbed-over bite mark that he had glued on, complete with freshly dried blood makeup. "It would be a waste on me."

"I neeeed to know they aren't poison." The boss's slur was returning, his moment of sober clarity passing.

"I just don't want to waste an injection," Joe said. The boss just stared at him, not budging. "How about I inject one of the girls? You'll see it's not poison, and I won't waste an injection." The boss nodded.

Joe took one of the needles filled with dyed saline out of the case, walked over and grabbed Kira's arm. "Don't worry, it will be okay," he said as he injected her with the solution. Everyone watched Kira for a few minutes. She was unharmed. Joe turned back to the boss. "See, sir."

The boss waved over his shoulder to the muscle-bound behemoth. The boss whispered to him, a little too loudly, and Joe could hear him. "Take him to the fighting pits. With the shot, he should last longer and make us more. Oh, and make him fight the other girl first. Turn her, and make that man kill her. As for the other girl, we'll figure out something to do, with her being immune to the zombies." The boss laughed with an evil grin as the big man nodded.

The boss lowered his gun and heightened his tone, obviously fake. "You are freeeee to go. This man will essscort you out. Pleeeease don't ever let me see any of you again."

"Thank you, sir." Joe extended his arm out, and the girls walked to him. He hugged Kira quickly. The man by the door opened it. Joe and the girls walked out, being trailed by the giant man.

Kira whispered, "Joe, there is no way he's letting us go."

"I know. When I tell you, reach down my pants."

Kira looked at him, confused.

"Trust me, and be careful when you pull it out."

As they exited the box, Joe led them, turning left toward the elevator. Joe laughed loudly and threw an arm around each girl, pulling them close. Joe spoke loudly enough so the man behind them would hear. "Girls, I'm so glad we made it out of here. Let's go home, NOW."

Jolie was confused by the way he was talking. She was about to ask why he was yelling, but she was cut off by what she saw next. She watched as Kira reached down Joe's pants, digging deeply. Jolie was in shock. She nearly gasped as Kira started to pull something out of his pants. She was so surprised that she couldn't look away as Kira pulled, inch by inch, a long, black knife from Joe's privates.

As soon as the knife was clear of his pants, Joe stopped, halting the whole group. He took a loud, deep breath. "Let's just take this moment in, girls."

"Keep moving," the man behind them commanded.

Joe held the group in place. "Just soak this in for a second, girls."

The man put his hand on Joe's shoulder, pressing into him to make him move. "Move."

Joe yelled, "NOW!"

Kira twisted under Joe's arm, stabbing the knife into the man's stomach.

Joe spun and used his leg to clip the back of the man's knee, causing him to fall. Joe jumped around the length of the man's body and wrapped him in a headlock, bending him while holding a rear choke hold.

Without pause, Kira jumped on the man, grabbing the knife. She pulled it out and started wildly thrusting, stabbing him again and again and again, until the man stopped moving. She turned the blade with one final twist as Joe released the choke hold. Kira pulled the knife out, and Joe rolled the man to the side. Joe picked up the AK-47 the man had dropped in the struggle.

"I'll need that knife," Joe said. Kira handed it back to him. He checked the rounds in the AK to make sure one was chambered. "We aren't out of this yet. Let's go before someone finds the body."

Kira and Joe started to walk toward the elevator. Jolie was frozen, staring at the man's bleeding body on the floor. "Jolie, come on," Joe said in a loud whisper. Jolie, still in shock, stepped toward the body and kicked it. "Come on!" This time, Joe said it through gritted teeth. Jolie shook her head, knocking the cobwebs out, and turned, running now with Kira and Joe.

"Keep going," Joe said as he ran past them. "We can't use that door at the bottom without using his key." About ten feet down from the elevator door, they entered the stairs.

Joe and the girls ran down the stairs. At the bottom, Joe stopped them. He wrapped his face with a piece of camouflage fabric. "Okay, from here we walk slowly. There are three guards down here, who are not expecting us. I need them not to react immediately, so we are going to make it look like you two are my prisoners. I'm the guard. You're the captives. And you're not happy about it, so I need you both to hold your hands behind you, like they are tied, and start crying."

Jolie and Kira both looked at each other and then at Joe. "We're kinda all cried out," Kira said.

"I'm sorry for this," Joe said. He slapped both girls' faces, hard. Tears instantly rose in their eyes. Jolie started crying a little. The look on Kira's face was one of pure betrayal. It cut through Joe's hard exterior and pricked his heart. That look hurt worse than he could let on right now. He hit her again, feeling the pain himself, but he needed her crying. Instead she steeled her runny eyes into an angry, determined look. *That will work too, I guess,* he thought. "When the gunshots start, drop to the floor. Now let's go." He turned the girls around and pushed them forward through the door, forcefully. The crying girls being led by a masked man was an image the door guards had seen before. In the dim lighting, they couldn't see that Joe's outfit was slightly different. The men were cautious but not instantly alerted.

A man by the elevator door and the man sitting in the chair by the garage door chains stood, aiming rifles at them. "Stop!" the man near the elevator yelled.

"Relax!" Joe said. "Boss killed the guy. He said that he wanted to teach these girls a lesson. Said that he was going to let all his men have their fun with them before he threw them out." Joe stood behind the girls, wondering if his ruse worked. The third man, who had been sitting in the security office, stepped out.

"Why haven't we heard about this on the radio?" he asked

"Boss passed out after giving the instructions," Joe said, thinking quickly.

The man replied, "Give me a second to check on this."

Joe needed to act now. "Check all you want, but take the girls off my hands! I have to take a shit."

The man at the security office nodded to the two men. Joe pushed the girls forward. As the two men advanced to grab Kira and Jolie, they lowered their weapons. Joe took the opportunity, raised the AK and fired first into the man walking at the farthest distance. The girls dropped at the sound of gunfire, just as planned. Joe spun the rifle and aimed at the second man, who only had time to turn his head before rounds opened his chest.

Joe aimed his rifle next at the security office. The man had dove inside after the first shots. Joe lit the office up while moving forward. He peppered it with short bursts of shots. "Move!" Joe yelled to the girls. They ran to get behind a cement pillar. Joe sprinted to the other side of the room, firing the last shots the AK had into the now-shattered glass of the security room. He got low and peered around the door. The man was still lying on the ground with his hands on his head, scared of the gunfire.

Joe jumped on him, pulling his knife out and burying it into the back of the man's skull. *Sorry for stabbing you in the back, but you shouldn't have touched my family.*

Joe walked out of the office and kicked open the entry door. Kira and Jolie ran past Joe, and soon they were all jogging away from the arena. Joe stopped them about thirty feet out of the door and retrieved his guns from the trash dumpster. "Hold up. Okay, girls, get to the boat. If I don't make it there by morning, leave without me."

"Where are you going?" asked Kira.

"There is something I have to do," Joe responded. "I can't let that piece of shit get away with this. He deserves punishment, and I'm going to give it to him. No one comes after my family and lives to talk about it. He is going to pay." Joe fired a shot into a window across the road. It shattered into a hundred pieces.

"Joe, we should go," Kira said

"I can't."

"Joe, please," Kira pleaded.

A group of men came around the corner on ATVs. They were all dressed in black combat suits and wearing gas masks. They rode right up to Joe, Kira and Jolie. One hopped off and threw a gas mask to Joe. "Get to the boat," Joe said to Kira as he caught the mask and checked his handgun.

"Come on, Kira," Jolie said, grabbing her by the arm.

Joe didn't look Kira in her eyes. He couldn't.

"Come on, Kira!" Jolie pulled on Kira's arm. The two girls took off running.

"So what's the plan?" the soldier asked Joe.

"The loading dock is clear. Come on," Joe said. The group ran inside. Joe ran up to the man nearest the elevator, lying in a pool of his own blood. He rummaged through his pockets until he found what he was looking for, pulling out the elevator key.

Joe and six other men all piled into the service lift. He turned the key and pushed the luxury-box floor. Joe slid the mask on over his face. "No one shoot the boss. I have special plans for him."

The elevator doors closed with a hiss of air.

New Miami Harbor: Outbreak Day +69

Joe walked up to the back of the yacht. The boss and all his main men were dead. Joe knocked on the locked door. No one answered. Joe had a moment of panic. Then he remembered he hadn't used the pattern.

Knock-knock-knock . . .

Knock . . .

Knock-knock-knock-knock.

A few seconds later, Kira opened the door. The look on her face almost killed Joe. She was an emotional mixture of fear, happiness and sadness.

Joe hugged her

Kira stayed silent, hugging him.

"I should have come with you," Joe said.

"What happened?"

**The Boss's Luxury Suite:
Outbreak Day +69**

Joe and the men lined up on either side of the double doors. Joe was on the front of one of the two columns of men. He and the other front man opened the doors slightly and tossed in tear-gas grenades and flash bangs. Four muffled explosions went off. Random gunfire followed for a few seconds. A few rounds burst through the wall above Joe. After a few seconds of silence, they infiltrated. The men cleared the room with military precision, using short, controlled bursts until all the men guarding the boss were dead. Rounds of ammunition had ripped through walls, couches and flesh. The only man left alive was the boss himself. He was sitting on the floor in the middle of the room, coughing, choking and crying. Joe pointed two fingers toward the bathroom door, and two men went to it. They opened the door and fired rounds into a man hiding behind the toilet.

Joe barely heard the shots as he walked up to the boss. His focused anger was about to be let out. He saw the boss reaching for the pistol shotgun he had dropped at some point in the fray. Joe grabbed it before the boss could.

"Fuck you!" the boss screamed.

Joe took off his gas mask, and the remnants of tear gas burned his eyes. Joe didn't care, as he wanted the boss to see his face. A little pain was worth it. Joe used "The Judge" against the boss, firing a .410 shotgun round into the boss's foot. Fat, skin and bone disappeared, a giant hole left.

"Ahhhh!" the boss yelled, bending over but unable to reach his foot, his stomach getting in the way.

Joe started laughing, an evil taking over his mind. "Ha ha ha. Look at you! You fat fuck!" Joe shot the boss's other foot too.

"Ahhh!"

"I'm sorry, does that hurt?" Joe yelled at him.

The boss yelled back at him. "Fuck you!"

"That's only a small amount of the pain you've inflicted on people! You!" Joe started hitting him with the butt of his gun as he yelled. "You! Piece! Of! Shit! You! Are! A! Waste! Of! A! Human! Being!" Sweat beaded down Joe's face as he kept hitting the pathetic image in front of him. Exhaustion finally stopped the bludgeoning.

Joe stepped back, looking at the crying, bloody and bruised pile of man. Joe regathered himself and caught his breath. He walked over to the metal case resting on the kitchenette bar top. Opening it, he pulled out a syringe

"This isn't actually an immunization. This is Enerjax. Who has the enhancer?" Joe asked the room. One man, still wearing his mask, stepped up holding out a metal cigar tube. As Joe reached for it, the man spoke.

"We should just end this."

Joe grabbed the tube from him. "It ends when I say. That was the deal." Joe opened the tube and pulled out an enhancer syringe. He walked over and stabbed him with the Enerjax. The boss quickly began to convulse, his fat jiggling. Then it all stopped. Joe walked over and, using his knife, cut the boss's Achilles tendons and wrists deeply.

A few seconds later, a scream came tearing out of the fat man's throat. The boss zombie was born. His head snapped up, and his white, milky eyes popped open. As he attempted to rise and attack Joe, who was closest to the creature, the cut Achilles caused his massive form to fall to the ground. The zombie boss tried to push up, but the cut wrist tendons made his hands unable to function.

Joe watched as the fat zombie blob tried to crawl toward him, but his weight held his body to the ground.

Joe watched him spit and struggle.

"Look at him," Joe said.

"Sir?" the man who gave him the Enerjax-enhancer needle asked.

"Now he looks like the monster he really was."

"Sir. Let's be done with this," the man said.

Joe walked up and injected the large creature with the enhancer. A few seconds later, the boss began convulsing again and then fell still, this time for good.

Joe fired one shot through his skull just to be sure.

New Miami Harbor: Outbreak Day +69

"Let's just go get Kurt and leave this place behind, and never talk about what happened in that room."

"Okay," Kira said. "This has been a long day, huh?"

"Yeah."

Transatlantic Convoy:
Outbreak Day +70

The sun was rising over the horizon as the go-fast boat came sailing out of the convoy again. Joe slowed down the *La Vida Dulce*. The voice of the security man from earlier chirped over the radio.

"Welcome to the Transatlantic Convoy, Captain Feller. We've received your permission from the mayor. Follow this boat, and we'll get you into formation."

"Roger," Joe said over the radio.

Kira was standing next to him. "Let's go find your brother."

Joe thought, as he pushed the throttle forward, *Kurt, I'm coming, man. I'm coming.*

To be completed in…

REBIRTH

About the Author

Jon DeLeon is a science-fiction author, CrossFit Level 1 Trainer and online marketing professional from Wellington, Colorado. For years DeLeon has enjoyed and loved science fiction, apocalyptic, fantasy, and action & adventure books, movies, and miniseries. DeLeon found himself swimming with story ideas and a desire to share them. After a few years of writing practice and story structure training, DeLeon is excited to have begun releasing his original stories.

New World is the second of a three-part book series titled Undead, all part of a series called The Apocalypse Chronicles.

To learn more about Jon DeLeon and his upcoming releases please visit:

BeyondNormalBooks.com

If you'd like to follow Jon DeLeon on Instagram you can find him at:

@jonathanrdeleon

Made in the USA
San Bernardino, CA
26 July 2018